After the Dust
Settles

GATLIN FIELDS

Sandra
Waggoner

Especially for Emma! :)
Sandy Waggoner
John 14:1-3
From Grandpa Bob
& Granny Love

Sable Creek
PRESS

Cover and text design by Diane King, www.dkingdesigner.com
Maggie photo by Deb Minnard; model Amanda Sheppard
Cover photo of house composed of photos © Ken Cole | Dreamstime.com and © Ann Cantelow | Dreamstime.com
Back cover photo © Tomislav Pinter | Dreamstime.com

Scripture taken from the King James Version. Public domain.

Published by Sable Creek Press, PO Box 12217, Glendale, Arizona 85318
www.sablecreekpress.com

Publisher's Cataloging-in-Publication data
Waggoner, Sandra.
    After the dust settles / Sandra Waggoner.
    p. cm.
    "Gatlin Fields"
    ISBN 9780982887516
    Summary : A jury verdict, a hasty promise, and a visit to the Gatlin mansion bring far different results than Maggie Daniels expected.

[1. Depressions--1929--Kansas--Fiction. 2. Family life--Kansas--Fiction. 3. Fathers and daughters--Juvenile fiction. 4. Christian fiction. 5. Revenge--Fiction.] I. Title.
PZ7.W124135. Af 2010
[Fic]--dc22   2010934611

Printed in the United States of America.

Chapters

A Verdict

"All rise."

The jury filed into the jammed courtroom. The crowd held its breath.

"You may be seated."

Tension was high. As people took their seats in the courtroom, only the whispered rustling of their clothing broke the silence.

Maggie's eyes slipped to Mr. Thomas Gatlin. She thought he looked relaxed because a smile played at the corner of his lips. Maggie shuddered. Just how could he be so confident that the jury would find him innocent? What if they did? What would happen to Maggie? Would she ever be free from feeling Thomas Gatlin lurking in the shadows every time the sun headed toward the western sky?

Mr. Thomas Gatlin must have felt her gaze because he turned slightly. He gave her a smooth nod, and the hint of a wink tiptoed at the corner of his eye. Cold chills seeped through Maggie's body. She leaned a little closer to Daddy so she would feel the warmth of safety.

"Has the jury reached a verdict?" the judge interrupted Maggie's thoughts.

Maggie watched the jury. Most of them kept their eyes on the floor, on the wall, or anywhere but on Thomas Gatlin. Maggie hoped this was a good sign.

The jury foreman stood, slid his sweaty hands down the sides of his pant legs, and then clasped his shaking hands together. "We have, Your Honor."

The judge nodded. "On the charge of kidnapping, what does the jury find?"

The foreman swallowed, and Maggie watched his Adam's apple bob up and down his scrawny neck. It reminded her of the tom turkey clinging to Cecil's back a few weeks ago. Then the man swallowed again and slipped a look at Thomas Gatlin. Swiping his sleeve across his forehead, the foreman opened his mouth, but he uttered no sound.

Judge Waldeman cleared his throat. "Wendle, as the foreman of the jury, you need to answer my question."

"Yes, sir, Judge Waldeman. It's just kind of hard." Again, Wendle nervously wiped his hands on his pant legs.

Judge Waldeman spoke calmly. "Wendle, all I'm asking you to do is let us know the decision the jury made. We don't need your feelings. Now, let's try this again. Has the jury come to a verdict?"

"Yes, Your Honor."

Judge Waldeman proceeded. "Well, Wendle, on the count of kidnapping, what does the jury find?"

Wendle's eyes looked as though they were about to pop out of his head. Again, he swallowed hard, but this time he didn't glance at Thomas Gatlin. "We, the members of the jury, find the defendant, Mr. Thomas Gatlin … " Wendle paused, gulping a breath of air as he struggled to continue, "We find Thomas Gatlin guilty as charged."

A gasp swelled through the courtroom.

Mrs. Crenshaw wailed. "Oh, Thomas! Of all the nerve. It can't be."

Thomas Gatlin dropped his mouth open in disbelief. He yanked his hand from his pocket and used his pointing finger as a whip toward the jury. "Wendle! I'll have your store for this!"

The color drained from Wendle's face while his Adam's apple pumped up and down, like the pipe on a windmill, to get the oxygen flowing again. Other members of the jury stole glances at each other and avoided Thomas Gatlin's line of vision. The strum of emotions in the courtroom raised the noise level to a crescendo.

Judge Waldeman took the gavel and pounded the wooden podium. "Order in the court! Order in the court!"

Thomas Gatlin shook. "All of you owe me! George Harless, Malcom Smith, Marvin Sivert, all of you!"

Louise Crenshaw held her purse high. "You all owe Thomas! Why, he is the reason you still have your houses and your stores and your farms! You should all be ashamed!"

"I will foreclose on each and every one of you!" Gatlin threatened.

"Silence!" Judge Waldeman slammed his gavel down. "Sheriff, if Thomas doesn't keep his mouth closed, you'll have to escort him back to the jail."

"Yes, sir, Judge Waldeman," the sheriff tipped his head and stepped closer to Thomas Gatlin.

Thomas Gatlin's lawyer pulled on his client's arm and pleaded with him to sit down. Thomas yanked his arm away and growled at his lawyer.

Mrs. Crenshaw glared. "You can't take him from the courtroom, Judge! It is his trial!"

Judge Waldeman frowned. "Louise, sit down, or I'll have Sheriff Ary remove you, too."

"How dare you," Mrs. Crenshaw hissed through clenched teeth.

"I dare fine, Louise. I'm the judge."

Chuckles were heard throughout the courtroom. Mrs. Crenshaw's face turned a light shade of purple. She leaned over the rail in front of her. "Some people think that just because they have a position, they can do whatever they want. I'll have you know when Thomas gets out of this … this … this mess, he'll have your job."

The judge turned to Mr. Crenshaw. "Arnold?"

"Sorry, Judge. Louise, sit down."

Louise's eyes sparked. "Arnold Jack Crenshaw!"

"Louise, later you can thank me. Right now you had best sit down, or you will be in contempt of the court." Arnold took her arm and sat her down.

"Thank you, Arnold." Judge Waldeman smiled and turned back to the jury. "Now, on the charge of attempted murder, what does the jury find?"

"We … " Wendle's voice squeaked, and he was forced to swallow and start again. "We, the jury, find Mr. Thomas Gatlin … guilty."

With a wild roar, Thomas Gatlin jumped over the table in front of him and dove toward Wendle. He grabbed the foreman by his shirt collar, pulled him over the banister, and threw him on the floor. Thomas dropped on Wendle's belly and started slugging. Jurors in the front row slunk back in horror while the crowd rose and surged toward the two men on the floor.

A newspaper reporter shoved through the crowd and began snapping pictures.

"Order in the court!" Judge Waldeman shouted. "Order in the court!" He slammed his gavel on the bench where he sat.

Sheriff Ary stepped behind Thomas and yanked him off Wendle. "Someone help the sheriff," Judge Waldeman ordered as Thomas turned toward Sheriff Ary.

Wendle rose to his hands and knees. Blood streamed from his nose. "I'll be glad to give the sheriff a hand."

"Good." Sheriff Ary twisted Thomas Gatlin's hands behind his back. "Wendle, get the handcuffs from my belt, and we'll get him secured."

The foreman took the handcuffs, clasped them on Thomas Gatlin's struggling wrists, and then pulled his handkerchief to swipe the blood from his nose. A drop splattered Thomas in the face as he twisted to challenge Wendle.

"I'll kill you for this! I promise I'll kill you," Thomas Gatlin spat at Wendle, gritting his teeth.

The sheriff smiled. "That will be hard to do from a jail cell, Mr. Gatlin."

Judge Waldeman threw his hands in the air. "That's it. Sheriff, take the defendant from the courtroom."

Wrestling in the aisle, Thomas set his feet and wedged himself against the bench. He thrust his face toward Maggie and planted his searing eyes on her. "I did not kidnap you. It was Stub Huggins. Just tell the court that!"

Maggie glared right back at Gatlin. "Stub Huggins kidnapped me because you told him to, and he was not the one who hit me on the head with the shotgun. You did that. Then you helped him throw that dirty gunnysack with me in it onto the train. And I heard you say you hoped I was dead!"

Thomas Gatlin pushed to lean in closer. "This is not over, not by a long shot. I promise you that."

Maggie grabbed her daddy's hand and slid behind him, out of Gatlin's reach. She was glad this evil man was going to jail. She hoped he would never get out. Still, his promise that things were not over chilled her to the bone.

Every time the *Dodge City Daily Globe* photographer clicked a picture with his camera, the flash blinded Maggie.

Daddy's deep voice broke in, "Sheriff, I would like to press charges against Thomas Gatlin for threatening my child."

"Sam," Sheriff Ary assured, "Maggie is safe. Mr. Gatlin is going nowhere but to the inside of a jail cell." Sheriff Ary moved his prisoner toward the door.

Sam nodded, "But for the record, I will be pressing charges."

Judge Waldeman pounded his gavel. "You can press the charges with me, Mr. Daniels."

As Thomas Gatlin was shoved down the aisle, Mrs. Crenshaw shouted, "Thomas! We will get you a better lawyer!" Then she turned and crossed the aisle to Maggie. "You brat! You liar. You horrid child. To think the people of this town believed you, a nothing, over Thomas Gatlin. You just wait until we get a better lawyer!"

Maggie was shaking.

Elbert squeezed between Maggie and Mrs. Crenshaw. "Maggie didn't lie. She never tells a lie."

Mrs. Crenshaw's eyes dropped to Elbert. She snatched his ear and twisted.

"Eeow!" Elbert tried to squirm away from her clutches.

Mr. Crenshaw stepped across and faced his wife. "Louise, this is enough. Let Elbert go."

Mrs. Crenshaw eased her grip, and Elbert scooted behind Maggie and her daddy.

Firmly, Mr. Crenshaw took Louise's arm and pulled her farther away from Maggie. "Louise, the girl has only done what is right."

"Right? You call that right?" Mrs. Crenshaw's cheeks were splotchy.

"Yes, Louise, I do."

Mrs. Crenshaw shook her head in disbelief. "Arnold! You are standing against me?"

"Louise, I am standing for right, for truth, and for justice. Thomas was wrong, and you know it. He may be your cousin and your hero, but he was wrong."

Louise sagged and fainted dead away. With her silenced, the stunned crowd turned their attention back to the judge. He pounded his gavel, and the spectators eased down onto their benches. Judge Waldeman looked over the people and cleared his throat. "Well, thank you, ladies and gentlemen of the jury. Wendle, I hope you are all right."

Wendle dabbed at his nose. "I think I'll be fine. Thank you, Judge."

"Good," Judge Waldeman sighed. "In all my years of court, I've never seen a verdict that got a reaction quite like this one. Because of this turn of events, we will have the sentencing at a later date. I will need to confer with both lawyers in my chambers. The rest of the courtroom is dismissed." Judge Waldeman gave his gavel a final blow, rose, and left the courtroom.

Maggie still clutched her daddy's hand. Her heart was racing, and she thought she would never forget Thomas Gatlin's face shoved within inches of her own.

Sue knelt and wrapped her arms around her frightened daughter. "Are you all right?"

The warmth of Sue's hug calmed Maggie's shivers. She nodded. "But I'm glad Opal and Ruby stayed with Mrs. Valina, because if they'd been here, they'd be having nightmares tonight."

"Yes, they would. I hope you don't, Maggie."

Maggie hoped she wouldn't, either. She'd have to do some talking to the God up in heaven tonight.

The Threat

As they walked down the steps of the courthouse, Maggie squeezed between Daddy and Sue, holding tightly to both their hands. The *Dodge City Daily Globe* photographer blocked their path and shoved his notebook in front of Maggie. "Young lady, how did you feel when you heard the guilty verdict for Mr. Thomas Gatlin?"

Maggie looked straight at the reporter. "I was glad."

The reporter continued, "Do you have any question at all as to the guilt of Mr. Gatlin?"

Maggie shook her head. "No, sir."

The reporter narrowed his eyes just a bit. "Young lady, are you sure you are not helping to send an innocent man to prison?"

Maggie swallowed. "Mr. Thomas Gatlin is not innocent."

For a moment, the reporter drummed his fingers on the side of his camera. "What were your feelings when Mr. Thomas Gatlin spoke to you in the courtroom?"

Maggie licked her lips. "I … I was scared."

After the Dust Settles

"Do you really think Mr. Thomas Gatlin can get you from behind bars?" the reporter asked.

Maggie shot a look at her daddy. "I guess he can't, but there is still Stub Huggins."

"What about Stub Huggins? Where do you think he might be, young lady?"

"I don't know. I just know he's gone. I don't know how far away gone is, but I hope it's a long, long ways away. I wish he were behind bars, too," Maggie told him.

"Are you afraid he'll come back and finish the job he started?" The reporter's pencil was poised, waiting for an answer.

"Stub Huggins only did what Mr. Thomas Gatlin told him to do. If you want to know where Stub Huggins is, try asking Thomas Gatlin. If anyone knows, he does."

Gasps surged from the crowd gathered around Maggie and the reporter.

"That is quite an accusation," the reporter said firmly.

Maggie felt herself begin to shake. Stub Huggins would be behind every dark, shadowy corner in her life as long as he was on the prowl.

Daddy pulled Maggie closer and pushed the reporter's notebook aside. "My daughter is finished answering questions for today."

The reporter was persistent, "Mr. Daniels, is it true that your wife is heir to the Gatlin estate? Did you know that information when you came to Dodge City, and is that why you married her?"

"Mister … ?"

"Jones."

"Mr. Jones, if you'd been listening during the trial, you'd recall that no one except Mr. Thomas Gatlin had even an inkling of the Gatlin estate situation. I suggest you go back over the trial records so you can get your story straight." Sam stepped aside to go around the reporter.

"But, Mr. Daniels, isn't it possible that you knew…?" the reporter's voice dwindled as he noticed fire kindling in the eyes of Maggie's daddy.

Sam spoke in a clipped voice, "Mr. Jones, this is not the time or the place. Don't make me do something I may regret."

"Regret? Because you are a deputy? That gives you the right to do things you'll regret?" the reporter sneered. "You think you are the law and therefore above the law?"

It was clear to Sam that the reporter was trying to provoke them. Sam let go of Maggie's hand. He stepped down so he would be eye-to-eye with Mr. Jones. "I'll say this one more time. This is not the time or the place."

Sheriff Ary's voice broke in. "Charlie, Sam is my deputy. I hired him because he is a man of character. I know you might be a bit on edge with Thomas Gatlin being your cousin and you missing your chance with Sue, but you missed it. Sue is married to Sam. Let dead dogs lie, Charlie."

Charlie Jones spread his hands as if innocent of the accusation. "Sheriff, I'm just looking at all angles of the story. A lot of people in Dodge City don't want to believe anything bad about Thomas Gatlin. How can the headlines of the newspaper he himself owns report what happened in this courtroom today? When Mr. Gatlin gets out of this, we'll all lose our jobs. It won't matter if we're family or not."

The sheriff rubbed his chin. "Charlie, I just locked Thomas in a jail cell, and I sent for the doctor to check him out. Charlie, I don't see that Thomas is getting out of this one."

"Really?" Charlie Jones stood with disbelief written all over his face.

"Really, Charlie. Did you listen in that courtroom? Did you not understand? Thomas Gatlin was convicted of kidnapping Maggie and almost killing her. Do you really think kidnapping and attempted murder should be covered up because Gatlin is the big man in Dodge City? Charlie, you'll do best to write the news as it happened. Don't try to make things up, and don't try to cover things up. When you slant facts, they're no longer facts. It'll get you into trouble."

Charlie removed his hat and slapped it against his leg. "Sheriff, reporting the truth can cost me my job." Charlie's shoulders sagged.

Sheriff Ary placed his hand on the reporter's shoulder. "Just report the facts. Leave the opinions out of it. People should be smart enough to draw their own conclusions."

The newspaper reporter shrugged.

Sheriff Ary motioned toward Sam. "My deputy is a good man, Charlie. I'll stand by him. Oh, and a little food for thought. If Sue is half owner of the Gatlin estate and you write that story, I'll bet Sue can fire you. Remember, Thomas Gatlin will be in jail. Since Sue is half owner of the newspaper, I guess that puts her in charge."

Maggie giggled as she watched the reporter soak in what the sheriff had just said.

Charlie Jones tucked his pad of paper and pencil into his pocket. "It was nice to meet you, Mr. Daniels. Maybe we could get together at another time and another place."

Sam nodded. "Another time and another place it is."

The reporter thanked Sam, tipped his hat at Sue, and continued down the courthouse steps two at a time.

"Sorry about that, Sam." Sheriff Ary put his hand on Sam's shoulder. "I'm afraid this town has been run by Gatlin a long time. It might take the people awhile to get used to change."

"You sure it's wise to keep me as your deputy, Sheriff?"

"Actually, I think it's better. You don't know enough people to be biased, and I believe you're the man for the job. By the way, we work too closely for you to be calling me 'Sheriff' all the time. Please, call me Paul."

"Thanks, Paul. I think I'll go pick up my two little ones and take the girls home. It'll probably be about an hour before I get back," Sam told the sheriff.

"Take the rest of the afternoon. It'll be good for the family. I've got to bring the books up to date. I need to hang around the office anyway. Besides, it might be better if you and Thomas Gatlin were not in the same building." The sheriff winked.

"Well, if you don't need me, I think I'll just take you up on that offer." Sam turned to Maggie and Sue. "How about it, ladies?"

Sue answered, "I would love it." She took Sheriff Ary's hand. "Thank you, Sheriff."

As they headed for the buckboard, Sam asked, teasingly, "Sue, what did the sheriff mean about that reporter missing his chance with you?"

Sue's cheeks burned crimson. "It was a one-time soda. He caught me in the drugstore and bought a fountain drink for me. That's all. He wanted a date, but I didn't. It's as simple as that."

"Mmm," Sam grinned. "Sue, are there any more beaus that will be crawling out of the woodwork?"

Sue paused just a moment too long.

"Maybe we had best talk about this at home, or, better yet, I'll just ask Opal and Ruby." Sam lifted Sue up to the wagon seat.

"Don't you dare. The less they know about those things, the better. However, I will say, I latched onto the best man." Sue traced her finger along Sam's cheek.

Maggie felt as if she were an intruder. She stepped up on the wheel and was ready to dive into the bed of the wagon when her daddy caught her about the waist. "Maggie," he swung her in a circle, "what a wonderful day this is. You will never have to worry about Thomas Gatlin again."

The click of the camera halted Maggie and Daddy's celebration dance.

Daddy pulled Maggie close and held her tightly. "Mr. Jones, you go right ahead and take a picture. This is one happy little girl with her daddy, and you can be sure, Mr. Jones, that Sue and I will read the caption."

"Yes, sir." Mr. Jones turned and left for the second time.

Daddy laughed and tossed Maggie into the back of the wagon. "Let's go get Opal and Ruby."

As they made their way down the street, Maggie noticed people stopping to stare. Some even whispered to each other and pointed in her family's direction. Maggie wondered if she would ever feel at home in Dodge City, Kansas. Then she remembered the boxcar. When Maggie had first found out it was to be her home, her heart had felt cold and empty. Now, even though it was old, run down, and small, it was cozy. Maybe the people made it cozy. Opal and Ruby were fun, even if they got into gobs of trouble. Their home rang with laughter. Warmth and love blanketed the boxcar. There were Opal, Ruby, Daddy, and her new mama, Sue. It was a true home.

The horses turned and started up the hill to Mrs. Valina's place. At the top of the hill was the gate to the Gatlin pasture they were forbidden to cross. Would things change now, since Sue owned half of all the Gatlin estate? Maggie remembered the first time she ever set eyes on the Gatlin mansion. It was the biggest, most beautiful house she had ever seen. Her heart had skipped a beat as she mistakenly thought it was to be her new home. Was it a possibility now that Sue was half-owner? In wonder Maggie breathed, "Wow, oh, wow!"

Maggie closed her eyes and let her daydreams fly. She could live in that mansion. She could see herself sitting on that amazing wrap-around porch. She would sit on the rail and lean against a big white pillar, and maybe she would be wearing a store-bought dress. Maybe the dress would be a bright Christmas plaid with mostly red, and she could have the hat of her choice. Maybe …

Daddy pulled Ben and Maude to a halt at the gate, and Maggie's eyes flew open, ending her daydream. Martin approached with his wide, toothless grin and swung the white gate open in welcome. "I been watching for you. Come on 'round back. Valina done made up a strawberry pie."

"That sounds wonderful, Martin," Sue laughed.

Maggie remembered the time Martin had cracked the whip at them before the dust blizzard had hit. He had told them Mr. Gatlin wouldn't let them cross the pasture anymore. Then Mrs. Valina, Martin's wife, had come and sweet-talked him into letting them through the gate because the storm was rolling in. Now, both Martin and his wife were very dear friends. Maggie had learned from Mrs. Valina about heaping coals of kindness, and about calling Sue "Mama."

Opal and Ruby ran to meet them, tumbling through the gate. Mrs. Valina followed.

"What happened?" Opal asked excitedly.

"Did Mr. Thomas Gatlin get guilty?" Ruby chimed the question.

Maggie jumped from the bed of the wagon. "He sure did."

Opal and Ruby clasped her hands, and together they danced in circles.

"You're free! Mr. Thomas Gatlin will never bother you again!" Opal shouted.

Maggie laughed, but she shivered inside as she remembered Thomas Gatlin's face glaring at her in the courtroom.

Valina held out her arms and scooped Maggie into a warm embrace. "Good news. Good news. Come on in and share some of my strawberry pie."

Maggie loved the special place of Mrs. Valina's arms where she was folded into the warmth of safety. Just let Mr. Thomas Gatlin try to get her there.

Warm Milk

I t was late when Maggie finally crawled in bed. Opal and Ruby didn't even go through their regular ritual of fighting. They had snuggled together and fallen asleep the minute their eyes closed. Maggie didn't. When her eyes closed, all she saw was Mr. Thomas Gatlin's face pushed toward hers, and she could still hear him saying it was not over yet. Impossible. Mr. Thomas Gatlin was in jail. It had to be over. Of course, Mrs. Crenshaw had said she would find a better lawyer. Maggie figured Mrs. Crenshaw would try, but she hoped it wouldn't change anything.

Maggie kicked the covers off. It was hot even for August. She slid out of bed and tiptoed to the window to make sure it was open all the way. They needed all the breeze they could get. The window was open as far as the window stick would hold it open. They needed a longer window stick. Tomorrow she would look for one. Maggie knelt at the window. Maybe she would just sleep here for tonight. She crossed her arms on the windowsill and laid her head down. A soft breeze stirred the cottonwood, but it was so hot the leaves were too tired to dance. They drooped and clumsily bumped into each other.

"Maggie." The soft breeze seemed to whisper her name, and Maggie smiled at the thought.

"Maggie," the breeze crooned. Her eyelids began to droop.

"Maggie." A tiny rock clinked on the windowsill where she rested her head. Maggie held her breath and put her hand over her heart. It couldn't have been the breeze that chucked the rock. Did that mean it was not the breeze after all that had seemed to call her name?

"Maggie." This time another tiny rock flew through the window, except this time it didn't land on the windowsill, it thumped her on the head. No breeze could have done that. Maggie perked her head up and searched the softly blanketed night.

"Maggie?"

Had she heard that voice before? Her lips trembled. "Who's there?" she asked in a whisper.

"Maggie, it's me, Jed. I got to talk to you. You got to come and help me."

Maggie's heart beat a bit faster. The last time she had gone out in the night, Jed's dad had thrown a shovel at her like a spear. Maybe Jed was trying to lure her into the night for his dad.

"Please, Maggie. I helped you. You got to help me." Jed's voice sounded desperate.

"What do you want?"

"I don't want anyone to hear us. You got to come outside," Jed begged.

"Are you alone?" Maggie was afraid Stub Huggins would stuff her into a gunnysack again.

"Yes, I'm alone," he whispered.

"Promise?"

"Promise. Cross my heart and hope to die."

"Okay, and you will keep that promise if anything happens to me!" she vowed low enough even Jed could not hear. Maggie moved through the room like a shadow, whisking through the quilted doorway and padding over the kitchen floor to the outside door. With a prayer, she eased it open and shadow-walked over the porch. Quietly she pulled the screen door closed and ran barefoot to the side of the boxcar. "Jed, what do you want?" Maggie asked.

Jed pulled at the loop on the leg of his faded overalls. "I need food. Any food will do. Maybe some biscuits and milk. My little brother, Jess, is sick."

"Why me? What about your pa? Why can't he get the stuff?"

"Pa ain't around. You know he'd gone straight to jail if he'd stayed around here. He's a wanted man."

"You mean your pa left Dodge City? He didn't take you and Jess with him? He left you and your brother alone?"

Jed shrugged. "He left us the scattergun. Besides, what else could he do? If he stayed, he'd be arrested, and the state would take us. They'd put a kid like me in an orphanage or a work-house, and I ain't goin' to no orphanage or no workhouse!"

"Jed, you got any relatives? You could go to them. We'd help get you there. Honest, we would."

Jed spread his hands. "Pa left kin behind 'cause he wasn't in too good a standin' with them. Besides, they don't want us 'cause they got enough problems of their own."

"Are you staying at your home place?"

Jed kicked the dirt. "No. N-O. No. That would be the first place the sheriff would look. I can read signs like an Indian trackin' a snake over the desert rocks. That sheriff's been checkin' on the place about every other day. In fact, he keeps comin' and pokin' around lookin' for Pa. He almost caught me day before yesterday."

Maggie looked Jed straight in the eye. "Where are you staying?"

"I can't be tellin' you that. Your daddy is the deputy. He'll come take us away and try to make us tell where my pa lit out to. Maggie, I just need some food. I think I need some warm milk for Jess. He's got the fever and a cough. I thought warm milk might help him out."

Maggie nodded. "We've got some biscuits on the table, and I'll get a jar for some milk. Do you have a way to warm it up?"

Jed shook his head. "I got to be careful about a fire in that dugout. It fills with smoke. Besides, if somebody sees the fire, they might find us. Jess, he's sort of scared of strangers."

Maggie squinted at Jed. "You're staying in a dugout?"

Jed groaned. "You got to promise me you won't tell nobody! I helped you out of a mighty tight spot. You owe it to me! Just forget the dugout." Jed was near panic at the slip he had made.

"Jed, I promise, but there has got to be a better place. A dugout is damp and dirty. That is not good for a sick kid. You don't want Jess to die, do you?" Maggie was scaring both of them.

"No. That's why I came to you. Please help me." Jed clutched at his heart.

Maggie didn't want Jess to die. "Okay. Stay put, and I'll be right back." Maggie tiptoed toward the porch, reached for the screen door, and eased it open. She took a deep breath and crossed the porch, passing through the house door toward the table where the biscuits were. She made a pocket by gathering the ruffled hem of her nightgown and quickly dropped the biscuits in it. She took a quart jar from the shelf. Maggie was glad Sue always stored the jars with the lids tightened firmly. Those lids would have made a lot of noise if they had been piled in a drawer.

Maggie scooted back outside to where Jed was waiting and motioned to her gown full of biscuits. "Here. Put these in your pockets."

Jed didn't have to be told twice. He stuffed his pockets full.

Maggie handed the jar to Jed. "Come on."

Jed held the jar to the moonlight. "Hey, this jar is empty."

"Yes," Maggie explained. "Jess needs warm milk, and I am not sticking around to light the stove. We're going to go get some warm milk from Lulubelle, our milk cow. Come on, she's in the shed."

Together they headed for the lean-to shed. Maggie was glad the full moon lit the barn, even though the moonlight made eerie shadows. At least she could see. Lulubelle was dozing, but she snorted when Maggie's hand grabbed hold. "It's okay, Lulubelle," Maggie soothed her. The milk rang as it hit the glass and steamed a bit as it began to fill the jar. Maggie continued to talk softly to Lulubelle so she would stay calm.

Ben and Maude stamped.

"Quiet, you two!" Maggie hissed.

Maggie turned to Jed. "See if you can keep them calm. If they make too much noise, Daddy will wake up and come to check on things."

Jed eased between the two horses. "Whoa," he patted them. Ben fidgeted, stepped to the side, and bumped into Maude. Maude whinnied and shot into the air, kicking the old milk cow. Lulubelle swished her tail over her backside, and Maggie dove out of the way before Lulubelle could kick. Maggie steadied the quart jar of milk and very thankfully sank to her knees.

Jed ran, stumbled, and fell. He tumbled from between the horses, crawling on all fours. He finally stopped just behind Maggie, chest heaving. "Those are monster horses," he gasped as he grabbed his heart.

Maggie laughed. "I'm sorry, Jed. They don't know you. They are really nice horses—I guess if they know a person."

"You crazy? I coulda' been killed." Jed dropped flat on the ground.

Maggie set the jar on the dry grass. "No, you wouldn't have been killed."

Then Maggie shook her head. "Oh, oh. In all of the commotion, I lost the lid to the jar. Can you go back in the barn and find it for me?"

Jed looked at her in disbelief. "You gotta be jokin'. I ain't gettin' in with those animals again. They know you, not me. I'll hold the jar. You go find the lid."

Maggie giggled. "Okay, but I wish you could've seen yourself crawling out of the barn. It was funny."

"Funny!" In the dim moonlight, Jed picked up a small clod of dirt and threw it at Maggie. It hit her and then clunked down on the missing lid. As Maggie reached for it, she glanced at the house. A lamp sputtered and sprung to life in the kitchen. As quick as lightning she snatched the lid, then ran and grabbed Jed. "We gotta get. Daddy is coming."

Maggie crammed the lid on the milk and twisted.

Jed and Maggie only paused long enough to hear Sue say, "Sam, be careful."

"I'll be careful, Sue. I got the shotgun."

"Shotgun?" Jed squeaked.

Together Maggie and Jed slunk behind the barn, ran wildly through the pasture, climbed the fence, and sped toward the railroad tracks. The peace the full moon offered was lost as the two stormed farther from the barn, Daddy, and the shotgun. Maggie thought her lungs would burst, and all she could hear was her own pounding heart. Suddenly she felt the cold steel of the railroad tracks vibrate under her bare feet. The startled girl froze as a train whistle blasted through her heartbeats. The train's light glared as it bolted around the curve, heading straight toward her.

"Run, Maggie, run!" Jed shouted. Maggie shook. Jed flew back to Maggie, yanked her arm, and heaved. Together they tumbled down the side of the railroad bank and lay flat while train sparks splattered their faces. Long after the train rumbled away, Maggie caught her wind.

"That was close," Maggie sighed.

"Too close. What happened anyway?" Jed asked.

"I don't know." Maggie shrugged her shoulders. "I guess the light blinded me."

Maggie cradled the unbroken jar of warm milk as the sound of the train whistle echoed in the far distance.

CHAPTER 4

The Dugout

The moon was high in the night sky when Jed and Maggie reached the dugout. Maggie thought it looked more like a hole in the ground. There were a few cottonwoods growing near the dugout, which was carved in the side of the deep bank along the Arkansas River. The river was mostly dry from no rain and the continual beating of the hot sun. It was a wonder there was any water left in Kansas. "This is where Jess and you are staying?"

"It's the best hideout we could find."

Maggie peeked into the black hole. It was so dark, she didn't think she could see her hand in front of her face. Thick, dank air that smelled of mud and rot filled her lungs. "Can Jess see in there?"

Jed shrugged. "It's night. You ain't s'posed to see in the night, and in the daytime, light drifts in."

"Are there bugs?" Maggie gulped.

Jed chuckled. "There's a lot of 'em, but you ain't afraid. You couldn't be afraid of a bug after jumpin' off of a train goin' at least 50 miles an hour when you were kidnapped. That sure was somethin' I didn't think no girl would ever do. When Cecil told me you did that, I knew you was one girl with a mighty lot of spunk."

"Anything was better than that horrid gunnysack your pa and Mr. Gatlin stuffed me in." Maggie shivered with the memory.

Jed kicked at the ground. "Sorry. You still jumped off the train, though."

"I had help, you know. Cecil and Elbert both grabbed my hands and yanked me off that train."

Jed said with pride, "It still took a lot of guts."

If Maggie was afraid of bugs, she decided Jed would never know. "You go in first."

Jed hollered into the cave. "Jess, you can put the scattergun down. It's just Maggie and me." He turned to Maggie. "We might have to light a fire so's you can help me take care of him, or else we can drag him out here. What do you think?"

There was no way Maggie wanted to go into that dark place, but she hated the thought of dragging Jess if he didn't feel up to it. "You said if you start a fire it gets all smoky in the cave? It seems like it would make Jess cough a lot."

"Like he's dyin'."

Maggie twisted the jar of milk in her hands. "Then we'd better get him out here. The moon is pretty bright, so maybe we'd be able to see without a fire."

Jed nodded. "Okay, Maggie. Do you want to come and help me?"

The last thing Maggie wanted to do was go inside the black mouth of that cave, but she guessed if she was going to help Jess, she'd have to.

Staggering, Jess appeared, almost like a ghost, in the opening of the dugout. Maggie swallowed a scream, and Jed grabbed his heart.

"Don't sneak up on a guy like that!" Jed scolded. "You nearly gave me a heart attack."

"Sorry … " Jess bent over in a coughing fit. Jed latched onto his little brother in order to keep him from falling.

Maggie looked at Jed. "Let's get him set down."

Together they found a place on the hard ground and piled a bunch of dead leaves so Jess would have a softer place to rest. Maggie dropped to her knees and reached over to feel Jess's forehead. "He's burning up. He needs a doctor."

Jed snapped a dead, dry stick in two pieces and rolled them in his palm. "No. Doctors take money, and we ain't got none. Besides, those nice people of Dodge City would stick us in an orphanage or a workhouse. I done told you that ain't in my plans. Maggie, I need your help, and like I told you, I figure you owe it to me. I went out on a limb for you, and my pa gave me the beatin' of my life." Jed pulled up his shirt. "Look, if you don't believe me."

Maggie gasped and threw her hand over her mouth. Fresh scars laced his back like dead branches of a winter tree. She groaned. The wounds were healed over, but she bet he'd carry the scars in his mind for the rest of his life. "I'm sorry," Maggie whispered.

Jed lowered his shirt. "It ain't the first time, and I don't feel it much now. I'm not sorry I went out on that limb for you, Maggie. I think you're a pretty honest person, even if you're a girl. If you promise somethin', I know you'll stick to your word." Jed got up and walked around. Finally, he turned back to Maggie. The moon shone on his face. He looked as if he carried a load someone twice his age would have a hard time handling. "Maggie, you're different. I'm puttin' both of our lives in your hands. I trust you. You got to promise me you won't tell a single livin' soul."

Maggie wished she had Sue or Mrs. Valina here to help her make this decision. She knew a promise shouldn't be given if you didn't intend to keep it. It wasn't that she didn't intend to keep it, but what if it worked into a life or death situation? Maggie looked at Jess. This could be the very life and death situation she was worried about. Jess needed a doctor badly.

Jed squatted beside Maggie and looked directly into her eyes. "Please, Maggie. I'm beggin' you."

Maggie could see the hopelessness in every line of his rigid face. All she could do was nod, giving her word.

Jed shoved his hand toward hers. "Let's bind it with a shake."

Maggie stretched out her hand.

"Jed, let's see if we can get some of this milk down Jess." Jed held him while Maggie touched the quart jar to his lips. The boy drank a little, but it started him coughing again. Maggie tried holding a biscuit to his mouth, but Jess turned away. It was just as well. If milk made him cough, what would a dry biscuit do?

With coaxing, Maggie got Jess to promise to sip a little more milk. Finally, she turned to Jed. "Every hour see if you can get him to drink some more milk. You probably better eat the biscuits because you've got to keep strong so you can take care of Jess, and you better not drink from the jar of milk after Jess. You might catch what he has."

Jed nodded. "Thanks, Maggie."

"I'll leave some food behind the barn tomorrow for the both of you."

Jed swallowed. "Thanks."

"There's one more sure thing we can do to help Jess and you."

"What?"

"We can pray to the God up in heaven. He's the miracle worker, and it kind of looks like Jess needs a miracle."

Jed gazed into the star-studded sky. "I ain't never seen God. I don't feel right about talkin' to somebody I can't see."

Maggie pulled her knees up and wrapped her arms about them. "Well, I haven't seen Him face to face, but I know He's there because He is here." Maggie pointed to her heart.

Jed tipped his head to the side. "Are you crazy?"

Maggie shook her head.

"Then how did that God out there somewhere get in your heart?"

"I asked Him."

"That's it? You asked Him and what happened? Did He tear open your chest and jump into your heart? That don't make no sense."

Maggie giggled. "Not to us, but I know He is there. Just think a minute. If God picked up a hunk of dirt and made a man, do you really think He has to rip a person apart to get into his heart when God made that very heart in the first place?"

Jed spread his hands wide. "I don't guess He would, but how are you so sure that God is there?"

"Because I talk to Him. When I pray I ask Him to do things, and He answers my prayers. I may not like His answers, but He always answers them." Maggie explained.

"Like what?"

Maggie looked at the sky. "Well, for instance, I asked God to give Daddy a job even after everyone in all of Dodge City turned him down. Now Daddy has a really good job. That is how I know God is in me."

Jed nodded. "Okay, okay. Since you think God is in you, you do the talkin' for Jess. I ain't talkin' to somebody I can't see."

Maggie studied Jed and took a deep breath. She looked to the stars, closed her eyes, and prayed. "Dear God up in heaven, thank you for being in my heart. It feels pretty safe having you there. I'm asking on Jed's behalf for his brother, Jess. Jess is really sick, and we're just kids. We don't know what to do, but would you please show us? Then help no one to find Jed and Jess, and help me not to get into too much trouble. Thank you, God. Amen. Oh, God, could you start letting Jed see you a little bit?"

When Maggie finished, she noticed that even the bugs of the night were silent. Neither Maggie nor Jed wanted to break the quiet. Even Jess's breathing was easier.

Finally, Maggie reached out to Jed. "I got to be getting home. I hope they didn't find I was gone, or I'll be in a heap of trouble."

Jed's eyes grew round. "Oh, Maggie, I'm sorry. Will you get a beatin'?"

Maggie shook her head. "Not like you got. I'd sure be in trouble, though."

"You need me to walk you back?"

Maggie turned to the dark night and was tempted. It would feel good to have someone by her side. "No, I think Jess needs you more. Besides, I've got the God up in heaven right here in my heart."

Jed squinted at Maggie. "Is that s'posed to keep bad things from happenin' to you?"

Maggie swallowed, "Well, He helps me out of tight places."

Jed slowly nodded. "Thanks, Maggie."

Maggie stepped into the darkness.

"Remember the promise," Jed called after the only girl he had ever trusted.

"I remember, Jed," Maggie softly answered. How could she forget that promise? Already it laid heavily on her heart because Jess's life might depend on it. "Dear God up in heaven, HELP me, please."

Somewhere in the far distance a train whistle sounded. Maggie shivered as she thought about the train Stub Huggins and Gatlin had thrown her on after they had tied her in a gunnysack. The God up in heaven had helped her out of that tight spot, and He had used Jed to do it!

Missing Biscuits

I t was hot and dry. Any mud she had gotten on her nightgown from the dugout had dried, so Maggie dusted it off as best as she could before she snuck into the house. Her feet would be sore tomorrow from the barefoot adventure. Gently she sat on the edge of the bed and waited to see if Opal or Ruby moved. Nothing. Maggie lay down and dropped off to sleep.

A couple of hours later, though it seemed like minutes, Opal shook her. "Maggie, Maggie. Come on and get up. Didn't you hear Mama calling?"

Maggie rolled over and yawned. Her eyes felt puffy, and she sighed sleepily.

"You don't look so good, Maggie."

Ruby leaned her head over Opal, "Are you okay, Maggie? Usually you wake us up on Saturday morning." Maggie moaned.

Opal grabbed Maggie's shoulder and shook it again. "Remember, Mrs. Valina wants us to help her today."

"Yes, Maggie, remember? We're going to put dust sheets over all the furniture in the Gatlin mansion." Ruby's eyes sparkled.

"You'll love the mansion," Opal added.

Maggie pulled herself up as a thrill of excitement traveled through her body, pushing the sleepy cobwebs away. Since the very first day she had seen the Gatlin mansion, she had wanted to step inside of it. When it had been off limits, she had wanted to see it even more.

"Breakfast," Sue called. "Come and get it while it's hot."

The three girls tumbled from behind the quilted door in their nightgowns.

Daddy raised his eyebrows. "I know it's not breakfast in bed, but is it bed at breakfast, ladies?" Opal and Ruby giggled.

"We couldn't get Maggie awake," Ruby chimed.

Opal added, "I even shook her."

Sue wrapped her arms around Maggie. "She had quite a rough day in court yesterday. She probably needed the sleep. Maggie, if you want to go back to bed for a bit, it would be okay."

Ruby squinted, "Maggie don't want to miss seeing the Gatlin mansion, Mama."

"Doesn't," Sue corrected Ruby.

"No, she don't," Rudy repeated.

Opal put her hands on her hips. "What Mama means is that you are supposed to say 'Maggie doesn't,' not 'Maggie don't.'"

Daddy stopped the argument before it had a chance to grow. "Ladies, I don't care if it's doesn't or don't. I'm a hungry man. Let's eat."

Opal looked at him in wonder. "In our nightclothes?"

"Opal, is the food hot?" Daddy asked.

She shrugged. "I guess."

"Then let's eat it now. I have to go to work soon, and I'd rather have hot food in my belly," Daddy reasoned.

Sue laughed. "Breakfast it is." She turned to the girls. "And you three are invited to come to the table in your nightgowns this morning," she chuckled.

After prayer was said and the hot cakes passed, Sue looked at Daddy. "Sam, I was going to make you some bacon and biscuit sandwiches for lunch today, but the biscuits were gone. I found a few crumbs and that is all. I know there were probably half a dozen biscuits left from last night's supper. They were in a bowl right here on the table."

Maggie dropped her head toward her plate and stuffed a load of pancakes into her mouth.

Daddy's fork stopped in mid-air. "Mice?"

Sue shook her head and laughed. "I hope not. Do you know how many mice it would take to eat all those biscuits?"

"Rats?" Opal's eyes were huge.

Daddy chuckled. "Maybe the two-legged kind."

Maggie peeked sideways, and she could tell, even though Daddy laughed, he was thinking about something besides rats.

Daddy asked, "Did one of you girls get very hungry in the middle of the night?"

Maggie chewed her overloaded mouthful of food and shook her head. Ruby and Opal giggled.

"Girls, did anything wake you up last night?" Daddy asked.

Opal and Ruby answered at once. Nothing had bothered them.

Maggie swallowed. "Nothing woke me up." That was as close to a lie as she wanted to get. Nothing had awakened her because she hadn't been asleep yet when Jed threw the rock and hit her on the head.

Daddy studied Maggie's face. "Are you sure?" Maggie nodded.

"It's mighty odd, Sue. Remember last night when I went out to check on the horses and Lulubelle because something seemed to be stirring them up?"

Sue nodded. "Yes."

"I found a crushed biscuit on the ground between Ben and Maude. I wonder if someone has been poking around the place again." Then Daddy shook his head. "If anyone had come in the house and taken those biscuits, I thought for sure I would have heard it."

Sue put her hand on her husband's arm. "Oh, Sam, not again. Surely, someone can't be snooping around again. Everything has come out in the open. I can't think of one single reason why anyone would be sneaking around."

Daddy paused. "I can't think of a good reason." The table was quiet.

Maggie looked at the two pancakes left on the plate. She wished she could take them for Jed and Jess, but she didn't dare. Her heart seemed to be beating in her ears, and her stomach rolled. This must be what guilt felt like, but how could she get rid of that feeling? Maggie didn't believe she was doing anything wrong. She was just keeping a promise. Jed trusted her.

Daddy stood, grabbed his hat, and put it on his head. "Sue, I want you to walk the girls over to Valina's today. I don't want them going alone." Daddy paused. "And Sue, I want you to take the shotgun when you go. It will be safer going, and maybe Martin can walk you back home. I don't want you coming back without Martin and the shotgun. That way Martin can make sure no one was here while you walked the girls over to the Gatlin mansion."

"Sam, do you think that is really necessary?" Sue asked.

"You are heir to half of the Gatlin estate. There were quite a few unhappy people at the trial yesterday."

Sue held her hand to her throat. "Sam, Thomas Gatlin is in jail. There is not a thing he can do."

Sam stood, crossed to his wife, and gently took her in his arms. "Thomas Gatlin is in jail, but no one has seen hide nor hair of Stub Huggins. Stub is a wily old he–coon from the hills of Kentucky. He hasn't been caught for moonshining or any-thing else rumor says he's done. We know he was working for Thomas Gatlin, and we know they almost killed Maggie. I'll feel better if you take the gun."

"Hello?" Someone rattled the screen door. Maggie jumped. The conversation in the room had been so intense, she hadn't heard a soul.

Daddy crossed to the door. "Come on in, Sheriff Ary."

"I believe I will." The sheriff stepped through the door. "Sam, I told you to call me Paul. Remember?"

Daddy nodded his head politely. "Paul."

Sue motioned to her empty chair. "Sheriff, have a seat. There are a couple of pancakes if you would like them. I'll get you a plate."

Sheriff Ary looked at the pancakes. "A man would be out of his mind to pass up an offer that looks and smells so good."

So much for taking some pancakes to Jed and Jess, Maggie thought as she watched Opal and Ruby put the plate in front of the sheriff.

"Don't mind getting a plate, Sue. I'll just eat off of this one." He took a knife to butter them and then liberally poured syrup over the pancakes. As he stabbed a huge bite, he paused. "After you left yesterday, Judge Waldeman served a court order for Thomas Gatlin to be transferred to the Larned State Hospital for a mental evaluation."

"What does that mean?" Sue asked. The sheriff seemed deep in thought. It seemed to Maggie that everyone in the room held their breath as they waited for his answer. In fact, that piece of information might be the whole reason Sheriff Ary had come out this morning.

Sheriff Ary studied everyone around the table before he spoke. "What it comes down to is this. If Thomas Gatlin is found to be insane, then the verdict of guilty does not stand. Instead of going to prison, he will be admitted to the mental institute until he is pronounced well." Maggie's lower lip trembled.

Again, Sue asked, "Sheriff, does that mean Thomas Gatlin could get by with kidnapping and attempted murder scot-free?"

Sheriff Ary nodded with a look of regret. "Yes."

"Do you think he will?" Daddy asked what everyone wanted to know.

"Not if I were the doctor, but I'm not. It is up to the doctor and the good Lord."

Sam leaned back in his chair. "When does he go for this evaluation?"

"I put him on the train to Larned at 3 a.m. today." Maggie swallowed. Could that have been the train whistle she had

heard in the night—the whistle that sent chills up her back with memories of her gunnysack ride?

"How will you know if he got to Larned, Paul?"

"They'll send a wire when he arrives at the hospital. I'll check with them later." Sheriff Ary turned to Sue. "Mighty good cooking, Sue. Thanks. Thanks a lot."

With the last bite, Sheriff Ary pushed away from the table. "I guess we'd best be going, Sam. I'll tell you what. We'll stop by the telegraph office on our way to work."

At the door, the sheriff tipped his hat. "Thank you, ladies."

Daddy stepped out, then stopped and turned back inside the door. "Sue, I'll pick up a lock in town today. That way we won't have to worry about missing biscuits anymore."

All Maggie could think about was that she had told Jed she would put a bundle of food behind the shed for him tonight. Now Daddy would be watching like a hawk, and what if the law was to let Thomas Gatlin go free?

CHAPTER 6

The Gatlin Mansion

As Maggie walked, her tender feet reminded her of last night and the problem with Jed and Jess. Jess was really sick and needed a doctor. Maggie slipped a guarded look at Sue. Could she ask her what to do? Would that be breaking her promise to Jed? Probably.

Maggie bit her lower lip. It was hot, but that was not why she was sweating. Somehow, before tonight even, she had to come up with help for Jess without breaking that stupid promise she had made to Jed.

Maggie closed her eyes and silently begged for help from the God up in heaven. She tripped on a dry cottonwood branch and fell flat. A cloud of dust swelled around her body, and she thought for a minute that the pancakes she had eaten for breakfast weren't going to stay down.

Opal put her hands on her hips. "What are you doing, Maggie?"

"She fell down. Can't you see that?" Ruby frowned at Opal.

Opal glared at Ruby. "Well, yes, I can tell that. I just wanted to know why she fell."

"Girls, quit arguing over Maggie's fall." Sue laid the shotgun on the grass and knelt. "Maggie, honey, are you all right?"

Maggie sputtered dirt. Mixed with her spit, it had begun to taste a little like rain. She took a breath of dusty air and started coughing as she rolled over to face Sue. Maggie grabbed her tummy—she sure didn't want those pancakes to come up! "Yes, I guess I'm all right. I just wasn't watching where I was going."

Sue smiled. "It did seem as if you were in another world. Maggie, is there something troubling you?"

Maggie needed this exact question, yet instead of turning to Sue for help, she lied. "No, nothing is bothering me."

"Are you sure?" Sue asked.

Maggie wished she could just turn to Sue for the help she needed, but instead, she shook her head. She felt guilty, and that feeling sure bothered her. Yet, wouldn't she have felt even more guilt if she had broken her promise to Jed? If you have to lie to keep a promise, does that make it wrong? Yes, something was definitely bothering her. It could be the thing with Jed and Jess. It could be Stub. It could be Mr. Thomas Gatlin getting pronounced mentally well someday and excused from all charges. It could be all of those, but mostly it was the keeping of the promise she wasn't sure she should have given in the first place. One way or another, Maggie had to get this settled.

Sue gave Maggie that look—the look saying, I'll accept your answer for now, but I still think there is something you are keeping from me.

Sue stretched out her hand to Maggie. "Let me help you up."

When Maggie stood, Sue paused for a moment before letting go of Maggie's hand. "Maggie, if you are worried because

someone was nosing about our house, please don't. Daddy will take care of watching over us. Nobody is going to have a chance to hurt us."

"Thanks, Mama," Maggie nodded. In a way, it was just what Maggie was afraid of happening. She knew exactly who was nosing around their house. It was Jed. If Jed got caught, he would think she broke her promise. How could she get word to Jed? She had to let him know to stay away from their boxcar because Daddy would be watching like a hawk.

Opal and Ruby each grabbed one of her hands. "We'll help you so you won't stumble again," Ruby smiled.

Opal and Ruby jabbered until they opened the pasture gate and stepped onto Gatlin property. They crossed to the huge white-trimmed brick house with a wrap-around porch.

"Wow! Oh, wow!" Opal was in awe. "Just think, Mama, half of this mansion belongs to you." Ruby clapped her hands and giggled.

Maggie's eyes traveled from the porch up to a second floor balcony, then to a half-round stained glass attic window. She wondered how long it would take to explore the whole mansion. Smiling as she thought of what Opal had said earlier, Maggie asked, "Opal, which half do you think belongs to Mama? The top half or the bottom half?" Opal scrunched her face.

"What?" Ruby asked for Opal.

"Or maybe one side is Mama's, and the other side is Mr. Thomas Gatlin's," Maggie teased.

"I'm not sharing no house with Mr. Thomas Gatlin," Opal stated.

Ruby whispered again, "What? You mean we would have to live with Mr. Thomas Gatlin?"

Maggie and Sue shared a laugh before Sue answered, "There is no way we will live under the same roof as Mr. Thomas Gatlin, not even one night. The lawyers will work all of that out."

Valina stepped from the massive front door onto the shady, cool porch. "Whoa, Mrs. Sue. You don't need no scattergun to take over this property. Half of it already belongs to you." Valina's rich laughter rang.

"Valina, I just walked the girls over to help you this morning," Sue said.

"With a shotgun? Mmm, mmm. Our pastures must be gettin' mighty fierce these days." Valina shook her head. "That cow Lulubelle take out after you?"

Ruby looked at Mama. "Lulubelle? You would shoot Lulubelle?"

Opal came to her Mama's defense. "Believe me, Lulubelle can be downright mean at times."

"Not mean enough to shoot," Maggie explained and hoped it was true.

"No, not mean enough to shoot." Sue laughed as she continued, "However, there's been a time or two when she threw such a fit while I was milking that I have considered it."

Ruby was worried. "Really?"

"No, dear. I would never shoot Lulubelle." Sue stroked Ruby's cheek while she explained to Valina about an unwanted visitor in the night. She ended by saying, "So, I'll pick up the girls before lunch?"

"Oh, Mrs. Sue, let me have the honor of lunch with these young ladies. Then Martin or I'll walk them home. They'll be as safe as if they was in the arms of Jesus His own self."

"Thank you, Valina."

Valina waved Sue on. "You'll find Martin in the barn, Mrs. Sue. Now, you go have you some quiet time, and I'll go have me some fun time. Come on, ladies. We got work to do."

With reverence, Maggie swept up the steps and leaned against a huge white pillar. She stood in awe as she closed her eyes and dreamed of living in this majestic place. Again, that Christmas plaid dress she dreamed of having someday flashed before her eyes. Would it ever really happen?

Maggie heard Mrs. Valina talking to the God up in heaven as if He stood right beside her. "Well, I declare that poor lady, Mrs. Sue, got more troubles than a frog got warts."

Maggie knew how it felt to have troubles. She sure had some troubles of her own right now.

Mrs. Valina gathered the three girls and shooed them into what she called the parlor.

Maggie listened while Mrs. Valina explained why they were covering all the furniture with sheets. "With all the dust that's been a-blowin' in this here country, Mr. Gatlin's furniture would be covered with dirt from Colorado, or Nebraska, or Oklahoma, or Missouri, or whichever that wind decides to blow itself from." She chuckled at her own joke and continued, "Mr. Thomas Gatlin dug himself one deep hole, and that hole is going to be mighty hard to dig out of. That man is going to be gone for an awful long time. So long, in fact, that you girls won't be remembering how his face looks."

Maggie thought Mrs. Valina was wrong. Mr. Thomas Gatlin's face would be plastered on her memory forever.

"But can't we just show the whole house to Maggie first, Mrs. Valina? She's never been in it before," Opal pleaded.

Mrs. Valina looked at Maggie. "I guess any young lady would at least want to first get a good look at what she's going to cover up!"

"Let's go," Opal clapped.

Ruby grabbed Maggie's hand. "Come on, you got to see this."

Opal took charge. "We're going to start in the basement of this mansion and take you all the way to the top."

Maggie was in awe. In the basement was a walk-in cooler. Every day ice was delivered to keep milk and meat cool. To top that off, Mr. Gatlin had his very own set of bowling lanes down there. That was the first time Maggie had ever seen a bowling alley. The rest of the basement seemed to be a bunch of storage rooms, and they were downright spooky. In the corner was a big wooden bin catching coal from an outside chute.

From the basement, they went to the main floor. Mauve floral designs graced the parlor, but Maggie's favorite was the carved wood around the embossed metal ceiling tiles. Filmy curtains hung on the windows. Maggie imagined herself curling up on one of the window seats to read a book.

The kitchen was bright and displayed the luxury of a hand pump at the sink. The dishes all matched as far as Maggie could tell. All of the cabinets had embossed glass doors that looked sparkling clean. A white table stood under double kitchen windows adorned with lacey curtains.

"But that is not where Mr. Thomas Gatlin eats," Opal informed Maggie. "Come with me." Opal pulled her into the dining room. "Mama said that Mr. Gatlin always made her set this table even if he was the only one eating."

Maggie looked down the long mahogany table with carved chairs lining each side. The chair at the head of the table had armrests. Truly, this was a table made for company, and Maggie thought how lonely she would feel if she had to sit there all by herself.

"Come on, Maggie. Let's go upstairs. All that's left down here is an old library." Opal tugged at Maggie's hand.

"Library?" Maggie tipped her head. She liked to read, and books were hard to come by. "Let me see it."

Opal groaned, but Ruby came to her rescue. "I'll show you, Maggie."

The library doors were heavy wood. When Ruby slid them open, they disappeared into the walls. Maggie had never seen doors like these before, and she couldn't resist playing with them a bit before she went any farther.

Opal looked pained. "Maggie, let's go."

That was when Maggie saw the walls of books. Surely, Mr. Thomas Gatlin must be a millionaire. Books filled the shelves that stretched from the floor to the ceiling on three of the four walls, and there was a rolling ladder to reach the shelves that touched the ceiling. A huge desk sat in the very middle of the room. Against the fourth wall rested a matching set of an over-stuffed couch and two chairs. Gently Maggie touched a finger to the back of a book. Maybe she would borrow a few books, if Sue would let her.

With Ruby's help, Opal coaxed Maggie from the library to the next floor, which seemed to be all bedrooms and closets. Maggie counted five huge bedrooms, each displaying a different color. Ruby hugged the door of the yellow room as they left. "This room is going to be mine someday."

Opal laughed, "Or mine. After all, I'm older than you."

"That's not fair," Ruby whined.

Maggie came to her rescue. "I'm older than both of you."

Both girls gasped, and Maggie giggled. She really didn't want the yellow room because she loved the blue room with the biggest window seat. She thought their whole boxcar would have fit inside that bedroom. However, all of the rooms had double windows, which made the rooms sunshiny and way better than anything she had ever lived in before.

Maggie saw the droop of Ruby's lip. "Ruby, we could share the yellow room."

"Really? That would be great." Ruby slipped her hand in Maggie's.

"You two can go ahead and share. I'll have my own room. Now you just have to see the top floor," Opal beamed.

"The attic?"

Opal nearly glowed. "It isn't an attic."

"It isn't?" Maggie asked.

Ruby shook her head, bouncing her curls. "No. It's a … "

Opal slapped her hand over Ruby's mouth. "Ruby, she's got to see it to believe it."

The three girls ran up the wide staircase. When they reached the top, Maggie stopped and stared. An empty room with a huge, glossy wooden floor stretched before her. Stained glass windows flowed along the walls of the room. The front wall of the house had two side rooms with a center window between them overlooking the front carriageway. "What is this place?" Maggie asked in awe.

"It's a ballroom!" Opal shouted and listened to her voice bounce around the empty room.

Tenderly Maggie stepped onto the dance floor. Opal and Ruby yanked off their shoes and began gliding in their socks.

They twirled, swirled, and swung each other around the floor. Maggie could almost imagine the music playing. While Opal and Ruby danced and giggled across the room, Maggie knelt to feel the wood. It was waxed and felt as smooth as glass. Maggie's heart fluttered. To her, this seemed like a fairy tale world, with the colors of the stained glass glinting in the floor.

Maggie slowly eased through each color, pausing. She imagined she could feel the different colors caressing her face. She was drawn to the half-round front window, wanting to look out at the world through the spray of colors. Gently she crossed to the window to look at her world through the colored glass. The purple seemed as if twilight were falling. The yellows made the sunshine glow, and the reds gave a hint of something mysterious. Green made her heart ache. If only the rain would come and make the grass that rich green again. The blue had to be her favorite. With the added blue, the sky doubled its shade and seemed intense and stormy. Maggie decided she loved the stained glass windows more than anything else in the mansion. She reached out to finger the glass. It was rough and bumpy, but that was the very thing that broke up the light shafts coming through the window to shine on the floor, the walls, and the ceiling.

Maggie started to turn from the window when a movement below caught her eye. She stood still. Someone was just outside the carriage house pressed against the wall and inching toward the doorway. Maggie watched as that someone slunk through the open door and into the shadows. Maggie bit her bottom lip. She knew who that someone was, but what was he doing here? Maggie turned to Opal and Ruby. The girls were still having their own ballroom dance, so she decided not to even tell them she was leaving. She tiptoed across the wooden floor with its wash of colors reflecting from the windows, made her way to the staircase, and quietly slipped down the stairs. When she reached the main floor, she hurried across the front entryway and reached for the crystal knob on the huge door leading outside to the front porch. Something was going on, and Maggie intended to solve the mystery.

CHAPTER 7

In the Carriage House

*M*aggie stepped out of the mansion into the hot sun. Before she headed to the carriage house, she shaded her eyes with her hand and scanned the Gatlin grounds. No one was in sight. She made a beeline to where she had seen that someone disappear. As she stepped into the shadows of the carriage house, she paused to let her eyes adjust. On the rear fender of Mr. Gatlin's Hudson, she saw a handprint in the dust. "Yes," Maggie thought, "he was in here." She held her breath and listened. There was a back door, but Maggie didn't think he had gone out of it. He had to be inside. Finally, she called, "Cecil."

There was no answer.

Maggie hadn't seen Cecil and Elbert since before the trial had started because Mrs. Crenshaw felt it would be disloyal to her cousin, Thomas Gatlin. Even though Cecil and Elbert were only Mrs. Crenshaw's nephews, she refused to allow them to associate with Maggie. The boys were forever getting into trouble, but they had rescued Maggie from the train that Stub Huggins and Thomas Gatlin had thrown her on.

"Cecil?" Still there was no answer. "Cecil, I know you're here. I saw you sneak around the side. You might as well come on out."

Along with an old hubcap, Cecil dropped from a rafter overhead. "Maggie, you got to hide me."

"Hide you? From who?"

Cecil's eyes were wild. "From Aunt Louise, that's who."

Maggie shook her head. "Now what did you do?"

Cecil spread his hands wide. "Honest, Maggie. I ain't done hardly nothing. I'm scared to breathe. I think she hates my guts for helping you out of that train car. She keeps saying if you hadn't been around to testify, her cousin wouldn't even have been charged with kidnapping and attempted murder. Ever since they delivered that guilty verdict on Thomas Gatlin, I think she's gone a little crazy."

"How?"

"Oh, she keeps ranting and raving about when they find Mr. Gatlin innocent by reason of insanity, he'll come and straighten everything out. She wants me to tell the court I lied, and Mr. Gatlin had nothing to do with you getting put in that train car. She wants me to say it was all Stub Huggins's idea."

"But it wasn't!" Maggie shook her head.

"I know that, but Aunt Louise says Stub won't be in any trouble because he lit out of the country. She says it won't hurt a soul."

"Cecil, saying that would be a lie, and a lie is never a good thing," Maggie said.

"I know that, too. What you don't know is how crazy mad Aunt Louise is. It'd almost be worth the lie just so she'd leave me alone." Cecil put his hand to his head.

"Even if you did tell a lie like this, Thomas Gatlin wouldn't get everything back. If he's found crazy he couldn't be put in charge of anything."

Cecil leaned against the car. "Not the way Aunt Louise figures it. She says everyone would understand that the reason he went a little berserk was because he was accused of a horrible crime he didn't do."

Maggie leaned against the car along with Cecil. "It would be a lie. Can you live with that?"

Cecil shook his head. "Probably not, but life sure might be easier."

"It may be easier for you, but not for others. Just think what that would do to Jed."

"Jed ain't here. He's disappeared along with his dad," Cecil said.

Maggie wanted to tell him it wasn't true, but again there was that promise she had made. She took a deep breath. "What about your uncle Mr. Crenshaw? He's a really nice man," Maggie suggested.

"It won't work. Aunt Louise won't even talk to Uncle Arnold, so he's been staying away. Elbert and I have hardly seen him."

"Find him, Cecil. I know he'll help you."

Cecil shrugged his shoulders. "I don't even know where to look."

"You can't lie just to save your hide. If you do, they will call a mistrial, and Mr. Thomas Gatlin will be roaming free again. He doesn't like me, and he probably feels the same about you. Do you really think he'll leave you alone?" Maggie asked.

Cecil threw his head back, "I don't know, Maggie."

"You've got to stick to the truth, or no one will ever believe you again," Maggie pleaded. "Surely it can't be that hard."

"Really? Look at this." Cecil pulled up his pant leg. Red welts crisscrossed his legs. Some had broken open, and Maggie could see where blood had run and dried.

She gasped, "What happened?"

"Aunt Louise was teaching me a lesson. She said I had no respect. She said if I respected her, I'd be willing to lie for her."

Maggie didn't know what to say. She knew Mrs. Crenshaw's temper. Maggie remembered being shut in the Crenshaw cellar, but Maggie didn't think Mrs. Crenshaw could be that mean to her own sister's boys.

Cecil set his jaw. "Maggie, I can't go back to Aunt Louise. I ran away from her, and she's madder than a wet hen. I just can't go back."

Maggie whispered, "What about Elbert?"

"I'm planning to sneak in and get him tonight. Last I knew, Aunt Louise had Elbert locked in his room while she beat the tar out of me. He ought to be safe in there. If he's smart, he will lock the door from the inside so she can't get in."

"How about if you tell Sheriff Ary?" Maggie asked. "If nothing else, he could get you and Elbert back to your mother." Cecil kicked the ground and swallowed a lump in his throat.

"Cecil?"

"Maggie, you ain't heard. Mama ain't well at all, and the doctor doesn't know if she ever will be again. She can't take care of Elbert and me. Daddy lost the job he had, so he went somewhere back east looking for a job. He gave Aunt Louise custody of me and Elbert." Cecil turned to Maggie and groaned. "I'm dead meat. If I go back, I'm dead meat!"

"Cecil, oh, Cecil, I didn't know. I'm so sorry." Maggie laid her hand on his shoulder.

Cecil's laugh was bitter. "Aunt Louise said it was for the best. She said people would understand why I lied in my grief."

Maggie sucked in her breath. How could someone be so heartless as to use grief for her own benefit? Maybe Mrs. Crenshaw was a picture of somebody who didn't have the God up in heaven in her heart. Maggie took Cecil's hand. "Come with me. Mrs. Valina can make your legs feel better, and she might know what to do."

Maggie felt Cecil stiffen as his eyes grew wild. The door to the carriage house screeched wide and the shaft of sunlight was broken only by the shadow of Mrs. Crenshaw.

"I might have known," Mrs. Crenshaw hissed from behind Maggie.

Maggie cringed and slowly turned around. Mrs. Crenshaw stood with her hands on her hips. She clutched a buggy whip in one fist. Her face was livid, and a bead of sweat trickled down her forehead. Quickly she smeared it away. Cecil ducked behind Maggie.

"You can't hide behind that brat of a girl," Mrs. Crenshaw yelled. "Cecil, get started for home, now!" she screamed as she waved the whip.

"Sorry, Maggie, but I'm out of here," Cecil whispered as he turned, scrambled around Thomas Gatlin's Hudson, and sped out the back door. Mrs. Crenshaw started after him, but Maggie stepped in front of her. She didn't know what else to do. She just knew she had to help Cecil. His aunt pushed her to the side, but by then Cecil was flying across the pasture. Mrs. Crenshaw turned her anger on Maggie. "You no good for noth-

ing snip of a girl! I'll show you some manners!" She raised the buggy whip and snapped it against Maggie's leg.

Maggie sucked in her breath as the shocking sting spread through her body. Tears welled up, but Maggie would not cry. Mrs. Crenshaw raised her whip again. Maggie ducked beneath the woman's arm and ran. Maggie's leg throbbed with each racing step. If she could just make it to the mansion, she would be safe. Without even being aware of what she was doing, Maggie screamed.

Mrs. Crenshaw was right behind Maggie, yelling, "If you think you'll be safe in there, you are wrong! The door is locked, and I'll have you arrested for trespassing on this property!"

Maggie hit the steps, stumbled onto the porch, and fell. She didn't even take time to get firmly back on her feet. She lurched toward the front door, all the while screaming, "Help! Help!"

"There'll be no help for you!" Mrs. Crenshaw shouted.

Maggie's heart was pounding. The air she was sucking in seemed to rip her lungs apart. She had to get to that door. She just had to get there before Mrs. Crenshaw caught her.

Maggie felt the shadow cover her before she saw it. Mrs. Valina, like an angel from heaven, pushed herself between Maggie and Mrs. Crenshaw. "Do we have a problem?" Mrs. Valina's deep, calm voice asked, but Maggie could tell that voice was holding back a storm. Maggie felt the protection of God himself as she eased to her feet and hid behind Mrs. Valina.

"Yes, we've got a problem," Mrs. Crenshaw clipped her words. "Get out of my way. That girl has no business on this property, and I mean to see that she gets off of it."

"Mrs. Crenshaw, Maggie is my guest. She is helping me close down Mr. Gatlin's house. When she's done, I'll see she gets home safely." Mrs. Valina was firm.

Mrs. Crenshaw glared. "I'll have your job for this. You mark my words. I'll have your job!"

Mrs. Valina smiled. "Mr. Gatlin hired me. I guess that means he'll have to be the one to fire me, and that might take a long time allowing for where he is right now. Until then, I'll continue what I'm doing. I assure you, I'll be responsible for Missy Maggie."

"Insolence!" Mrs. Crenshaw spat.

"Yes, ma'am," Mrs. Valina smiled. Then she studied the angry woman. "I'm a bit worried about your health, Mrs. Crenshaw. You seem a little short of breath, and your face is mighty flushed. Would you like me to have my man, Martin, walk you home?"

"No, I would not." Mrs. Crenshaw was insulted. She pointed the buggy whip at Mrs. Valina. "I guarantee you, I'll notify Sheriff Ary."

Mrs. Valina nodded, "Yes, ma'am."

Mrs. Crenshaw ground her teeth. Maggie figured she couldn't think of something worse to say, so she turned and left. Maggie's whole body was shaking, and she was very glad when Mrs. Valina reached out and wrapped comforting arms around her. Opal and Ruby scudded from behind the front door, adding their arms to the hug. Tears streamed down Maggie's cheeks.

Opal was the first to talk. "She's gone now, Maggie."

Ruby stroked Maggie's hair over and over again saying, "It will be okay, Maggie. It's okay."

Mrs. Valina whispered, but Maggie overheard. "If that woman don't change her ways, she's got herself a place with her name on it right next door to Satan himself. Poor, poor Satan."

Chicken Broth & Honey

"I'm thinking we had better sit ourselves down for a bit of a snack before we cover the furniture," Mrs. Valina said. "That a ways Missy Maggie can rest awhile." Mrs. Valina pulled a chair from the kitchen table and helped Maggie sit down. Then she scooted another chair over to Maggie and propped her leg on it to examine the girl's wound. "I can 'most guarantee you'll not be working at the Crenshaws' when your mama and daddy see this leg. Mmm, mmm," Valina shook her head. "Why this here welt must be seven or eight inches long and fire red." Gently Valina wrapped a warm, wet towel over the welt on Maggie's leg.

Maggie winced. She knew Mrs. Valina was right about her mama and daddy not wanting her around Mrs. Crenshaw anymore. The bold fact was that Maggie didn't want to be around Mrs. Crenshaw either, but Maggie really did like being with Mr. Crenshaw. Then she remembered Cecil saying Mr. Crenshaw hadn't been at the house very much. If that were true, it would mean Cecil and Elbert would need her even more because Mrs.

Crenshaw would focus all her wrath on Maggie and leave the boys alone. Maggie grimaced. "I still want the job."

Opal's mouth dropped. "You'd still go to work for that mean, vicious woman?"

Ruby's eyes welled up. "She might kill you."

Maggie spread her hands. "Opal and Ruby, stop and think. Mama hasn't gotten money from the estate yet. Daddy's getting paid for being the deputy, but not enough to catch us up on the bills. We could still use the money," Maggie reasoned.

Mrs. Valina turned from the sink and stared at Maggie. "Child, do you know what you're asking for?"

Maggie's voice was shaky. "Mrs. Valina, I owe it to Cecil and Elbert." Maggie absently rubbed her fingers in circles on the top of the white table.

"Missy, you don't owe that family anything." Mrs. Valina pulled out a chair and sat across from Maggie.

Maggie swallowed. "Maybe not Mrs. Crenshaw, but I really don't work for her. I work for Mr. Crenshaw, and he is very nice to me. He kept Mr. Thomas Gatlin from taking Mama's safety deposit box, which held all those secrets. Then there is Cecil and Elbert. I think when I am at the Crenshaw house, Mrs. Crenshaw is nicer to them. Besides, Cecil and Elbert risked their lives to hop on that train and save me. They got me off the train, and Cecil carried me half the way home. Who knows where I'd be if they hadn't done what they did."

"Missy, the God in your heart is bursting forth, showing His own self for sure." Mrs. Valina shook her head. "Still I don't know if that mama and daddy of yours will allow you to be close to that woman. I'm afraid I wouldn't."

Maggie looked down at the tabletop. She wasn't sure she wanted to be that close to Mrs. Crenshaw either, but how else was she to help Cecil and Elbert? If Cecil did get Elbert out tonight and they ran away, she wouldn't have to worry about being there to help them. Maybe she'd just better pray for their escape.

Mrs. Valina reached over and patted Maggie's hand. "God His own self will iron out the kinks." Mrs. Valina turned to Opal and Ruby, "You two ladies come follow me into the pantry. Mr. Gatlin keeps it stocked plumb full. We'll go decide what we want for our snack."

Maggie watched through the door and listened to the giggling girls oohing and aahing. It seemed the pantry was wall-to-wall shelves stashed with food from floor to ceiling. Maggie heard Ruby's excitement over peanut butter and Mrs. Valina insisting on something hot for Maggie.

That was when the idea struck like a bolt of lightning. The Gatlin mansion would be the perfect hideout. Somehow Maggie had to get Jed and Jess into this house. No one would think of looking for them here. After closing down the place, not even Mrs. Valina would be in and out of it. The Gatlin mansion would be great for hiding. There was shelter, food, a water pump at the kitchen sink, and soft beds—probably better than Jed and Jess had ever had in their whole lives. Now Maggie had to figure a way to get to them and a way to get them here.

Mrs. Valina shooed the girls out of the pantry. Each carried her own goodies. Mrs. Valina told Maggie, "Missy, those two ladies decided to have peanut butter and honey sandwiches."

"Honey?" Maggie asked.

"You ever tasted honey, Missy?" Maggie shook her head.

"Then it'll be a first for you. Those bees make the sweetest sugar in the world, and it's downright good for you. It helps allergies, and it's the best cough syrup a body can get for a cough because the good Lord made it himself."

Maggie's ears perked. Honey helped a cough? She needed some honey for Jess.

"Miss Opal and Miss Ruby thought you'd want peanut butter and honey sandwiches, too. Now I surely don't care, but I pulled out a jar of chicken broth I canned last year, and I want you to drink a bit of it first. Chicken broth is about the best thing to calm a body down and to cure a sickness."

"Yes, ma'am." Maggie's mind was racing. Chicken broth would be exactly the medicine for Jess. She had to figure a way to get it to him. Maybe she could sip a little and ask to take the rest of the jar home. Later she would slip it out behind the shed.

Ruby was busy smearing peanut butter while Opal chattered, "I don't see why we have to throw sheets on Mr. Gatlin's furniture."

Mrs. Valina chuckled. "Ladies, Mr. Thomas Gatlin will be gone a long time, and we've been having these dust blizzards mighty often. Can you just imagine what his furniture would look like if we didn't cover it for when he comes home? Why, he'd drop on that couch in there and be lost in a dust storm right there in the middle of his very own sitting room."

Ruby giggled and Opal added, "I'd like to see that."

Mrs. Valina laughed as she poured the broth in a pan to heat. "Yes, that would be quite a sight, but I expect I'd be losing my job if it happened."

Maggie smiled while she listened to them talk. It was calming. Sisters gave her such a good feeling. She laid her head on the table and closed her eyes. Quickly they flashed open. That was it. That was how she could get her message to Jed and Jess. She would pretend to go to sleep, and then she would sneak out with the warm broth and the honey. Surely it would work. It had to work. Again she snapped her eyes closed, relaxed, and played like she was asleep.

Valina turned. "Well, now, would you looky there? That poor girl wore herself out, or could be Mrs. Crenshaw scared her near to death. Ladies, let's see if we can get her to the couch and just let her sleep for a bit. After we eat, we'll start upstairs with covering the furniture."

When they had Maggie settled on the couch, everyone tiptoed from the room. Maggie listened and prayed she wouldn't fall asleep for real. She had a nagging feeling in her heart that pretending was a little like a lie, but what else could she do? If she told anyone, it would be breaking her promise to Jed. Maggie began to hate that promise. It was like carrying doomsday in her pocket. Somehow, sometime, she was sure to spill the beans.

Finally she heard Mrs. Valina and the girls head upstairs. Maggie counted to sixty. Surely that would be enough time. As silently as she could, she slipped into the kitchen. She had to pour the warm broth back into the jar and put the lid on it. Then she scooped up the jar of honey. Maggie pulled open a drawer, picked up a spoon, and slipped it into her pocket. In no time she was out the door, off the porch, and running across the pasture. It was farther from the Gatlin mansion to the dugout than it was from her boxcar home, and Maggie had to hurry. She had to be back resting on the couch before the girls finished upstairs. She breathed a quiet prayer as she feared the thought of someone coming to check on her.

The day was hot and quiet. The only thing that stirred was the breeze through Maggie's hair as she ran. She stopped under the big cottonwood tree in their pasture. All the dancing leaves drooped, but the shade felt cool. Maggie's mouth was dry from sucking in air as she ran, and she wished she had a drink. She looked to where Lulubelle lay in the shade of the boxcar. Maggie didn't see a sign of movement, and she decided she had rested long enough. Again she took off running. When she reached the fence behind their shed, she stopped and carefully set the jars down while she climbed the fence. She looked longingly at the shed and wished she could leave the jars there, but she had to tell the boys about the hiding place. Then she reached under the fence for the jars.

Maggie heard the train before it came into sight. Her heart was already pounding from running, but it brought back the terror of being thrown in that empty boxcar. The frightened girl dropped to the ground, squeezed her eyes closed, and waited for the train to pass. She felt the vibration through her whole body. As the train faded away in the distance, Maggie lifted her head. She wondered if trains would always trigger her feelings of fear.

With a deep breath, Maggie stood and dusted off the front of her dress. She picked up her jars and crossed over the railroad tracks. She walked to the dry river and listened for Jed and Jess at the mouth of the dugout. Maggie couldn't hear a sound. She stepped to the gaping hole. "Jed," she called softly. No answer. Maggie took a deep breath and called a bit louder, "Jed."

There was still no answer. Maggie groaned. She hoped they hadn't been found. They were probably just so far inside the dugout they couldn't hear her calling. Would she have to go into that dark cave? She closed her eyes and decided she would try one more time. "Jed?"

Dirt crumbled from above and scattered all around her. Maggie looked up. Jed stood as still as a statue on top of the dugout with his finger over his lips. Maggie understood that meant for her to keep quiet. Ever so slightly she nodded.

Then Jed motioned for her to move, or maybe for her to hide. Frantically Maggie searched in her mind for a place to hide that wasn't in the dugout. There was nowhere else to go. Jed motioned again, only this time there was more urgency.

With a prayer, Maggie nodded. She sucked in a deep breath and stepped into the mouth of the cave. A musty smell arose, and she remembered that time she had been locked in Mrs. Crenshaw's cellar. Maggie forced her feet to take her further into the cave. She nearly screamed when she bumped into a heap on the dirt floor. That heap started coughing.

From outside of the cave she heard a voice she would never forget. "Jed, you ain't to tell nobody I was here. Do you understand, Boy? Not a single soul."

"Yes, sir, Pa," Jed answered.

"This will all be over soon, and we can get Jess a doctor. Until I finish this business, I want you to take care of your brother. Understand?"

"Yes, sir, Pa," Jed repeated.

Maggie didn't even know she was holding her breath, and it seemed like an eternity before Jed tromped into the dugout.

"He's gone, Maggie. He just come for the scattergun."

"Jed, what is he going to do with the scattergun?" Maggie asked. Jed paused. "Jed?"

"Pa said he had some unfinished business. He didn't tell me what, but I'm scared. I sure didn't want him to see you."

Maggie shivered as she thought she was probably his unfinished business. She guessed she was just about always in the wrong place at the wrong time.

Jed was the one to break the silence. "Maggie, I'll sneak you back after dark so Pa won't find you."

"I can't wait that long. If Mrs. Valina and the girls find me gone, everyone is going to be looking for me. I came to bring some chicken broth for Jess and some honey for his cough. Mrs. Valina says it's the best cough medicine ever."

Jed grabbed Maggie's arms. "You told her about us!"

"No, Jed. I promised you I wouldn't tell, and I keep my word. I'm scared, though, and I wish I hadn't made that promise. What if Jess dies? Just how are we going to feel then? It will be our fault."

"We can't let him die. You brought stuff to make him well, and you can always pray to your God. He helped you out of a tough time; maybe He will help Jess. Maggie, you have got to keep your promise. I am not goin' to live in no orphanage or workhouse," Jed pleaded.

Maggie dropped her head. "All right, I'll keep praying, but you can't come around my house anymore because Daddy found signs of someone snooping around. He's going to be watching really close the next few nights."

Jed laughed in a way that told Maggie he wasn't amused. "Oh, that's great, and you can't come around here anymore 'cause Pa will be back, and I guarantee he'll be watchin' close. For that matter, I don't even want to be here when Pa comes back."

Maggie reached out to Jed. "I have a better hiding place."

"Where?"

"Inside the Gatlin mansion."

Jed laughed. "Right!"

"Really, Jed. Mrs. Valina's covering everything with dust-sheets and locking up the place. No one is going to be around. There is a pantry full of food. There is running water and really nice beds to sleep in. It would be the best place to hole up and help Jess get better."

"Maggie, you just said they were lockin' it up. How are we s'posed to get in the place?" Jed wanted to know.

"It's a piece of cake. All you have to do is slide through the coal chute. You'll be locked inside and safe as can be." Maggie stopped. She could tell Jed was thinking over the idea.

Maggie reasoned, "Jed, it's got to be better than this dugout, and it would be a place where no one would ever think of looking for you two."

Jed was nodding. "Okay. Okay. I'll get this chicken broth down Jess, and somehow I'll get him there after dark. Thanks, Maggie."

"Sure. Listen, I'd stay and help, but I got to get back before they find me gone. They'll ask a lot of questions if I get caught," Maggie said.

"Thanks, Maggie. Be careful. Watch out for Pa. He's got the scattergun, and I am scared for you. Please be careful."

Maggie nodded. She was scared for herself, too. "You be careful, Jed."

Maggie turned and looked both ways before she stepped out of the cave. The daylight blinded her, and her mouth was even drier than the dirt beneath her feet. She was terrified, and she would be careful. Jed's Pa was somewhere, and if he was close, she would have to see him before he saw her. She hated the gunnysack Stub Huggins had shoved her in when he had kidnapped her. The gunnysack had been horrible, but Stub Huggins had the scattergun this time.

Knee-high to a Bullfrog

Maggie knew she was in trouble the minute she looked at the Gatlin mansion. Mrs. Valina stood on the top step with her arms crossed, her jaw set, and her foot keeping rapid time to a tune Maggie didn't want to hear. It was a troublesome tune all right. It was the same tune Daddy used when he wanted answers to questions Maggie knew would bring her a heap of trouble. Usually it ended with Maggie doing a bit of paddle dancing.

Opal ran to her side. "We've been looking all over for you, Maggie."

Ruby followed, "Yep. We was just going to find Martin to help us look."

Guilt melted all through Maggie. Keeping her secret was becoming more than she thought she could handle.

"Were you walking in your sleep?" Opal asked.

"Are you feeling better?" Ruby wanted to know.

Mrs. Valina hadn't said a single word yet, and Maggie was worried. Mrs. Valina always seemed to know what was going on inside her. Could she know Maggie's secret? Maggie nodded answers to Opal and Ruby, but she was wondering just what Mrs. Valina was going to ask. Slowly Maggie climbed the stairs. Opal and Ruby each seized an arm to help her.

Mrs. Valina smiled, but Maggie noticed her smile didn't quite reach her eyes. "That leg of yours must be a-doin' much, much better, Missy."

Maggie nodded. Mrs. Valina had always been her friend, and Maggie felt as if she had betrayed that friendship. Maggie hadn't really lied to this lady, but she had come pretty close. The feeling twisted in her tummy. This was not how a friend treated another friend. Maggie couldn't look Mrs. Valina in the eye.

Mrs. Valina stuck her finger under Maggie's chin and raised her face to look deeply into her eyes. "Mmm, hmm. Missy, you come with me. We need to have ourselves a little talk. Opal, you take Ruby and go help Martin in the garden. You tell him I said so. He'll understand."

Opal and Ruby only hesitated for a minute. They liked working with Martin. He gave them just about anything they wanted. Maggie understood Mrs. Valina, and she was afraid of the little talk they were about to have.

Mrs. Valina went to the door and held it open. "Come on in the kitchen. I don't suppose you've eaten—although I see that both the broth and the honey have disappeared."

Maggie let her eyes stray about the room. She didn't want to look at Mrs. Valina or anywhere near her. "No, ma'am."

"Well, you set yourself down while I dig out another jar of broth. You need something warm in that tummy."

Maggie hoped the something warm would stay down. Right now it would take a miracle. Maggie's guilt caused her tummy to roll in somersaults.

Mrs. Valina came back with another jar and began singing softly as she opened it and poured the broth into the pan. "'At the cross, at the cross, where I first saw the light, and the burden of my heart rolled away.'" Then she began talking, "Lord, those burdens were heavy—mighty heavy. They were more than I could bear. It pretty near made me feel guilty all the time. Why, I couldn't even look at my preacher."

Mrs. Valina pulled the drawer open and picked up a spoon. She opened the cabinet for a bowl and dipped broth into it. She swayed to the table and set the bowl in front of Maggie. Then she pulled out a chair for herself, sat down, and began to pray. "Dear Lord, we know you are a God that forgives us our wrongs when we ask, and we know you love us more than we deserve. Please, Lord, be with Missy Maggie's food," she paused before she added, "and her heart. Amen."

By the time Mrs. Valina was done praying, Maggie had tears rolling down her face. She couldn't even pick up the spoon, and there was no way she could swallow a bite. "Mrs. Valina, I'm sorry," Maggie sobbed.

Mrs. Valina opened her arms, and Maggie dove in them.

Mrs. Valina crooned. Finally she spoke, "Missy, I don't know what you done, but something is a-tuggin' at your heart. It seems to be a big, heavy burden. If I can help, I surely will, but you got to tell me how."

Maggie continued to sob, "I can't."

"Missy, you know that anything is safe with me, even a secret. We done been through this afore."

Maggie sniffed, "I know, I know, but this is a promise I made to someone else. I promised not to tell anyone. I can't tell you."

Mrs. Valina looked about the room. "Missy, I'm thinking maybe it was a promise made too quickly. Maybe it shouldn't have been made at all. Did you take time to pray about this promise before you made it?"

"There wasn't enough time to pray," Maggie wailed.

Mrs. Valina nodded her head. "Mmm, hum. I've done that before. It sure does make sleeping hard. Sometimes it can even make a person tell lies and hurt the ones they love the most."

Maggie looked at Mrs. Valina in wonder. How could she know what Maggie was feeling?

"Missy, in the Good Book it says you are to keep your vows. A vow is a promise, and it should be kept. The good Lord himself says in Numbers 30:2, 'If a man vow a vow unto the LORD, or swear an oath to bind his soul with a bond; he shall not break his word.' There are some promises made that should never be made, though, and deep down in one's heart, they know when they made a promise that is wrong. A wrong promise could end up hurting someone. It could even hurt the very one who made the promise. Nevertheless, a vow must be kept."

Mrs. Valina bowed her head for a moment before continuing, "Missy Maggie, you can keep your promise, but if there are things I can help you with, you need to let me know. Now, what can you tell me?"

Maggie swept her hands across her cheeks. "You already helped me, Mrs. Valina. You told me broth was good for most all sick people, and honey was good for a cough."

"Mmm, hum. So, I'm guessing somebody you know is sick?" Maggie nodded. Mrs. Valina pursed her lips together. "Does this someone have a fever?" Again Maggie nodded. "Does this someone need a doctor?"

Maggie swallowed, "I think so, but there's no money, and I already tried talking about a doctor. The answer was a big fat NO."

"Maggie, is this person as sick as your daddy was?"

Maggie shrugged her shoulders. "I don't know, but I'm worried about him. He coughs a lot like the way Daddy did. I'm scared he might die."

"Maggie, would he see me?"

"I don't know. Maybe I could talk him into it, but I really don't know. If he thinks I broke my promise, he'll hide from me. Then I won't be able to help him at all."

Mrs. Valina looked upward. "Dear Lord, we sure can get ourselves into a pickle sometimes. We need your help just now. I don't even know who I'm a-prayin' for, but you already got your almighty hand on him. Please take good care of Missy Maggie's friend."

A quiet settled in the kitchen, and Maggie could almost feel the God up in heaven surround them. For the first time, she thought Jess would make it and everything would work out for the best.

"Mrs. Valina, I'm sorry about pretending I was asleep. I felt awful, like I had told a whopper of a lie. I don't ever want to do that again," Maggie confessed. With the confession, Maggie could feel that black cloud being swept away, and she never wished to walk under that cloud again as long as she lived.

Mrs. Valina chuckled, "Those lies will do that to a child of God every time. As for me, you are forgiven, but I want you to learn a lesson from it. Don't ever promise until you have had time to pray about it. Remember, I'm a friend, and I'm here to help. I'm not your enemy."

"Yes, ma'am," Maggie whispered.

Mrs. Valina sighed, "Now, come give me a hug." Maggie jumped into those arms, and it was the best place to be.

The back door slammed. Mrs. Valina chuckled as Martin walked into the kitchen with Opal and Ruby clutching his hands. "Well, look what the cat dragged in."

A tiny grin edged at Martin's lips. "These young'uns told me there was peanut butter to be found in here, and they say they're hungry."

Opal reminded Mrs. Valina, "We were very hard workers today, you know."

Ruby giggled, "Yep, we sure were."

Mrs. Valina shook her head. "It looks like y'all are ganging up on me. What choice do I got but to feed the lot of you? I suppose Maggie wants some, too?"

Maggie nodded. Peanut butter was a very rare experience, and it would be wonderful. As they had their peanut butter party, the room bubbled with talk, questions, and fun. The Gatlin kitchen hadn't heard that much laughter in years. Maggie's heart swelled. Sisters, Mrs. Valina, Martin, and peanut butter were a combination she would remember forever.

When finally the last crumbs were gone, all the fingers licked, and the kitchen sparkling clean, they walked through the parlor to the front door. The parlor was dimly lit. It was much later than Maggie had thought. The sheets draped on the furniture gave it a ghostly look. The white coverings swayed as the group moved through the room, and it gave Maggie an eerie feeling. Chills ran up and down her back. She sure was glad she had Martin and Mrs. Valina close by.

Even though Opal and Ruby clasped Martin's hand and held on for dear life, they were explosive with mirth. Maggie noticed Martin's face split with a real smile joined by a chuckle. Maggie had never heard him laugh before, and the sound gave her deep down comfort.

When they stepped out on the porch, evening shadows were dancing. Mrs. Valina handed the keys to Martin. With keys jingling, he locked the door and turned, "All the other doors locked?"

"I do believe they are," Mrs. Valina answered.

"Then this house is safe and off limits to everyone, except to Mrs. Sue if she should want to come. After all, I guess Mrs. Sue is just as much the owner as Mr. Thomas Gatlin his own self." Martin patted one of the white pillars.

Maggie felt guilt tugging at her heart again. Her promise carried a load of weight. She reasoned it away because the Gatlin mansion was the safest, most unlikely place anyone would look for Jed and Jess. It would be better for Maggie, too, because she wouldn't have to keep sneaking out with food, and surely Jess would get well now.

At the gate to the pasture, Mrs. Valina leaned close to Martin and touched his cheek with a kiss. Opal and Ruby giggled. Mrs. Valina chuckled and batted the air with an open hand. "Oh, you young'uns go on now. Martin is my man, and I like my man. God gave him to me."

Even Maggie laughed while Martin turned three shades of red.

Mrs. Valina took turns giving the girls hugs. Along with Maggie's hug she whispered, "If your mama will let you come over after services tomorrow, I have a concoction that should help your secret friend get better."

Maggie gazed into Mrs. Valina's rich brown eyes. She couldn't find one bit of a grudge against her for the secret she held. Truly

Mrs. Valina was a friend from the God up in heaven. "Thank you, Mrs. Valina." Maggie hugged her tight.

Opal and Ruby had already claimed Martin's hands, so Maggie picked up a dead branch and trailed it behind as she followed. The girls jabbered, and once in a while Martin answered a question or two.

Maggie watched the sunset. Kansas had to have the most spectacular sunsets ever. If the sun had an identity, Maggie decided, she would have to be a rich lady. She always displayed colors in brilliant hues that gently flowed across the sky, and she decked herself in jewels. Sometimes she was so bright your eyes would hurt if you looked at her, and she was forever sparking light off of things that lay on the earthen floor.

Maggie heard a rustling and glanced at the big cottonwood tree. Lulubelle was still out. "Martin, I'm going to go head Lulubelle to the shed. She's got to be milked even though she never thinks so."

Martin nodded and continued with the chattering girls. "Do you need any help, Missy Maggie?"

"No. I bring her in all the time." Maggie walked, still dragging her stick. "Come on, Lulubelle. It's milking time."

When Maggie reached out to pat Lulubelle, she noticed a rope around her neck. Maggie tipped her head to the side. Daddy never put a rope on Lulubelle because for the most part, she was tame. "Lulubelle, how did you get a rope?" Maggie asked as she stepped closer to study the situation.

"Girlie," a hoarse voice sent chills through Maggie as she stood stone still in the darkening evening.

Maggie sucked in her breath. There was only one man that had ever called her Girlie. She turned to run.

"I wouldn't try it if I was you. I got this here scattergun aimed at ole Martin there, and I'm a right good shot. I ain't missed nothin' since I was knee-high to a bullfrog."

Maggie had found the voice, and she looked up into the tree. Stub Huggins did have a gun, and it was for sure pointed at Martin. "What do you want?" she said with her voice quivering.

"I want to know where my boys went."

"How would I know where they went? Everyone thinks they're with you," Maggie shrugged.

"Girlie, I got this feelin' you know exactly where they are. Now Jed took to you, and if anyone knows where he might be, I'm thinkin' it's you." Stub Huggins edged the barrel of the gun to cover Maggie. "Now, Girlie, tell me what you know."

"Mr. Stub," Maggie began. She took a step closer and swung the cottonwood branch she had been dragging in the dirt earlier, smacking Lulubelle in the behind. Lulubelle bawled and kicked the tree. Stub Huggins tumbled out of the cottonwood and to the ground. The scattergun belched fire toward the sky, showering Lulubelle with stinging pellets. Lulubelle snorted, danced a hoof or two on Stub Huggins, and raced toward the shed.

Stub Huggins grabbed his scattergun and his side. He stumbled to his feet and high-tailed it across the pasture.

Maggie's cheek stung. She wiped her hand across her face and felt warm, wet blood. A tiny pellet must have gotten her, too. Maggie rubbed where her heart was pounding a rhythm Stub couldn't outrun. Maggie laughed as she called, "Mr. Stub Huggins, I guess that is the first shot you've missed since you were knee-high to a bullfrog!"

CHAPTER 10

An Eastbound Train

All chaos broke loose. Stub Huggins flew with a high stepping limp across the pasture, over the railroad tracks, and to the dry Arkansas River. Opal and Ruby were screaming and dancing circles around Martin while he desperately tried to get to Maggie without hurting the other girls. Sue ran around the corner of the boxcar and was nearly knocked over by Lulubelle, the terrified milk cow. Maggie sank to the ground and lay in laughter. She would never forget the surprised look sprawled across Stub Huggins's face, or the words he spewed into the air when he landed on the ground. Maggie closed her eyes, and relief tingled through her body.

"Maggie!" Opal shouted and rushed to Maggie's side. "She's got blood all over her."

"Is she dead?" Ruby sobbed.

Sue dropped to the ground beside Maggie and gently lifted her by the shoulders. "Maggie, can you hear me?"

Maggie blinked as Sue, Opal, and Ruby surrounded her. Martin stood with his head slumped against the tree trunk, and

Maggie was sure he was crying. She assured Sue and the girls, "I can hear you just fine."

"She's not dead! She's not dead!" Ruby lay across Maggie and hugged her.

Gently Sue pulled Ruby away. "Thank the Lord she's not dead, but she may be hurt. We don't want to hurt her more." Sue studied Maggie, "Honey, where does it hurt?"

Maggie giggled. "I'm fine. My cheek stings a little bit, but I'm nowhere near dead."

Sue was puzzled. "Are you sure you feel okay?"

Opal bent over Maggie's face. "You got blood all over your cheek, and you keep laughing. That is not okay. People don't laugh when they're hurt."

Now Maggie burst into laughter. Opal backed away, and Ruby grabbed Opal's hand. Even Sue looked worried at Maggie's strange reaction.

Martin dropped his head. "It is all my fault, Mrs. Sue. I let Missy Maggie go get the cow. I should have gone with her." Nervously he twisted his hands back and forth.

Maggie sat up. "Martin, I'm used to getting Lulubelle. I do it all the time. Don't worry. I'm fine. I think I'm probably a whole lot better than ole Stub Huggins. He hit the ground pretty hard when he fell out of that tree, and then Lulubelle tromped on him a couple of times." Again Maggie giggled. "It was really very funny. That's why I was laughing."

Sue held Maggie. "Margaret Pearl, you gave me the scare of a lifetime." As Sue let her go she said, "Maybe we had better have Dr. Nelson check you out to make sure you're not hurt."

"Honest, I'm fine. Lulubelle may not be, and I'm pretty sure Stub Huggins is in pain, but I am fine."

Martin stepped closer. "Mrs. Sue, do you want me to go after Stub?"

Wildly Maggie shook her head. "Please, don't let Martin go after Stub. He's got a gun," Maggie begged. She had seen Stub with his gun aimed at Martin, and she didn't want her friend in Stub Huggins's range ever again.

Sue smiled. "I think that is a job for the sheriff, Martin. I'll bet he can handle it just fine."

"Are you sure, Mrs. Sue? I saw where he went." Martin plucked at his pocket.

Sue reached out to touch Martin's arm. "Then you tell Sheriff Ary where Stub Huggins went. If you want to walk on over to the house with us, the sheriff should be bringing Sam home pretty soon. I'd feel better, too, if you are with us the rest of the way to the house, and I'll bet the sheriff will give you a ride home. It's going to be dark soon, and I don't want you walking across this pasture alone in the dark."

"I guess I could do that, but Valina will start to worry about me." Martin looked toward home. "I sure don't want her to come looking."

Maggie looked at the sky and watched the first evening stars begin to twinkle. "I could run and tell Mrs. Valina."

A resounding "no" came from everyone in the group.

Sue took Maggie's hand. "You are not getting out of my sight tonight. Let's head to the house."

Before they reached the front door, Sheriff Ary's car pulled up.

Opal ran to the auto. "Daddy, Stub Huggins shot Maggie!"

"And Lulubelle," Ruby chimed in.

"What?" Daddy was out of the car and racing to Maggie. He knelt on the ground in front of his daughter. "Maggie?"

When he saw the blood, he pulled her into his arms and headed for the house. Sheriff Ary was right behind him.

Inside, Daddy sat in the rocker with Maggie on his lap. He looked closely at her face to get a good look at the wound.

"Daddy, I'm all right. It was just a little bit of shot from his scattergun. Mostly the pellets hit Lulubelle," Maggie told him.

Daddy's jaw twitched. "Where is Stub Huggins? I'll teach him to mess with my family." Maggie had seen that look in her daddy's eyes before when Thomas Gatlin had threatened Maggie in the courtroom.

"Sam, calm down," Sheriff Ary said. "We'll find Stub."

Martin stepped up. "I can show you where he run off to. I'd have followed, but I needed to make sure Missy Maggie was all right."

Sam nodded. "Good. That's what I wanted you to do. Thank you, Martin."

Sheriff Ary put his arm on Martin's shoulder. "Martin, making sure Maggie was all right was your first responsibility. You did a good job of it. Now, you said you could show us where Stub headed off to?"

Martin nodded. "I know exactly where he crossed the tracks and which way he headed on the other side. You want me to take you there?"

"Yes." Sheriff Ary looked at Maggie's daddy. "Sam, are you staying or coming?"

"If my girl here is all right, I'm coming. I can't wait to get my hands on Stub Huggins."

Sheriff Ary leaned against the stove. "Now, Sam, we have to do this legally. We can't go after Stub like a bull in a china closet."

Sam smiled, "Why, Sheriff, you know me. I wouldn't hurt a fly, but I want to be there to explain the law to Stub Huggins when we catch him. He needs to know his rights." Maggie couldn't help but grin at her daddy's words and the twinkle in his eyes.

Sue had gotten a washcloth to bathe Maggie's face. She stopped and looked into Sam's eyes. "Sam, don't do anything foolish. I don't want you to end up in jail alongside of Stub Huggins."

Sam chuckled. "That might be just the answer. One of the two of us wouldn't last very long. It might make for an interesting night."

"Sam, I'm not sure I find this amusing."

Sheriff Ary spoke, "Sue, Sam is just teasing. He's too good a man to stoop to Stub Huggins's level." Sheriff Ary turned to Sue's husband, "That is right, isn't it, Sam?"

The sheriff waited for Sam to nod before he continued, "Now, let's see just how much damage Stub has done to your daughter."

Maggie giggled. "Daddy, I'm better than Lulubelle and a whole lot better than Stub Huggins."

"How do you know that?"

"You should have seen Stub trying to run. He looked like a clumsy puppet on strings, and he was sure holding onto his side—probably from Lulubelle stomping on him a couple of times."

"Good ole Lulubelle." Maggie's daddy smiled.

Sue had finished cleaning the dry blood from Maggie's face. There were a couple of powder burns and one place on her cheek where the skin had been broken open. Sue folded

the washcloth. "Maggie, I'm sure God smiled on you today, and He must have a couple of angels with powder burns, too. I don't think we need Dr. Nelson. I believe you'll be fine."

Sheriff Ary squatted beside Maggie. "I want you to write down as much as you can about what happened today while everything is pretty clear in your mind. That way we can use it for trial. I'll pick up your statement later when I bring your daddy back."

"Yes, sir."

When Martin, Daddy, and the sheriff left, the ladies gathered around the table. It seemed that the day had gotten more and more exciting as it wore on. Opal and Ruby told about the peanut butter and honey sandwiches and claimed that would for sure be one of the main dishes in heaven.

Sue laughed. "Peanut butter and honey sandwiches in heaven? Well, I hadn't thought of it, but they would be quite nice."

Then they talked of the Gatlin mansion and the many rooms—especially the ballroom. Maggie added, "I love the stained glass windows. They are kind of like life. Some days are sunny yellow and some are stormy blue. They shine all over the floor and you just walk right from one color on to the next one."

Sue smiled. "You have quite an imagination, young lady. I think those windows are one of my favorite things about the mansion, too."

"Mama," Opal licked her lips, "do you think we will ever live in the Gatlin mansion? You do own half of it, don't you?"

"Opal, I don't know. The lawyers are still sorting things out, and I've asked Mr. Crenshaw to study the legal papers for

me. He understands things like that much better than your daddy and I do." Sue rested her chin on her hands.

Ruby smiled dreamily. "It makes me feel all like I've got bubbles in my tummy. I hope we get to live there. I'd pick out the yellow bedroom for my very own."

"You'd be too scared to sleep all by yourself," Opal told her.

"Sure, right now—because of all those sheets over the furniture. It's spooky," Ruby agreed.

"It was a lot of work with just Mrs. Valina, Ruby, and me," Opal blew the bangs of her hair as if she were exhausted from the hard work.

"And Maggie," Sue said.

"Maggie didn't help with the sheets," Opal said. Slowly Sue turned her eyes on Maggie.

Ruby explained, "Mrs. Crenshaw showed up and hit Maggie with a buggy whip, so Mrs. Valina made her lay down to sleep."

"What?" Sue asked with raised eyebrows.

Maggie's heart sank. She had hoped everyone would forget the Mrs. Crenshaw part of the day. She had almost forgotten herself.

"Maggie, I want to know what happened," Sue was firm.

Maggie took a deep breath and hoped she could keep Cecil out of the explanation. "Mama, Mrs. Crenshaw found me on the property, and she was chasing me off. She said I didn't have any right to be on the Thomas Gatlin place. Then she hit me with her buggy whip, and I took off running for the porch. Mrs. Valina saved me from her."

"Thank the Lord for Valina," Sue whispered.

Opal's eyes were huge. "But Mrs. Crenshaw told Mrs. Valina that she would for sure lose her job."

"Can she do that?" asked Ruby.

"No. She cannot do that. Valina was hired by Mr. Gatlin, and since I am part owner of the mansion, I would not allow Mrs. Crenshaw to fire Valina." Sue pressed her lips together before she added, "But Louise Crenshaw cannot go around hitting my daughter with a buggy whip, either."

Maggie had never seen Sue that mad before.

Sue continued, "That woman thinks she runs Dodge City. Well, she is going to find herself in a heap of trouble. Let me see where she hit you, Maggie." Maggie showed Sue her leg. The welt had gone down, but it had left a fiery red streak surrounded by hues of blue. "Maggie, I'm sorry. Opal, get another wet washcloth, please." Sue stroked Maggie's leg. "You must know this means you will not be working at the Crenshaw place anymore?"

Maggie dropped her head. Right now she didn't care if she ever saw Mrs. Crenshaw again, but she did care if Cecil and Elbert were okay. "I don't think she meant to hit me that hard."

"No, Maggie. I don't care what she meant. You are not going to work there one more day. That woman is not right, and I'm afraid you would not be safe."

"But … "

Sue cut Maggie off before she could make another plea. "The answer is 'no.' Your daddy will agree with me on this. He may even press charges. Mrs. Crenshaw had no right to hit you, no right at all."

Maggie could see she was getting nowhere. Maybe after they had slept and things had died down a bit, she could talk Sue and Daddy into it, or maybe Cecil had escaped with Elbert. Then she wouldn't even need to work for Mrs. Crenshaw.

Maggie thought about the Gatlin mansion and her plan to help Jed and Jess hide in there. If she had only thought about it when she had seen Cecil, she could have told him it would make a good hiding place for him and Elbert, too.

They heard Sheriff Ary's auto pull up to the boxcar and the doors slam. Opal was the first to ask, "Did you find Stub Huggins?"

"No," Sheriff Ary answered.

Daddy saw the worried look on all his girls' faces. "We traced him, though. It looks as if he jumped an eastbound train. You ladies won't have to worry about him anymore."

Sue had her hand on her throat. "I hope he did jump a train, and I hope it's one that takes him as far away as the Atlantic Ocean. I'd feel better, though, if you had him behind bars."

Sheriff Ary sighed. "An eastbound train. He's gone for now, but I still want that statement from Maggie. If he ever comes back, we won't waste any time. We'll get him right off the bat." Sheriff Ary tightened his lips and snapped his fingers in disappointment. "I sure wish we'd have gotten to him before he jumped on that train!"

Vows, Promises, & Deals?

"I hate walking into church late," Opal whispered to Maggie. "Everyone turns around and gawks at you. I wish they'd mind their own business."

Maggie felt about the same, but Daddy had insisted he put the lock on their front door before they left. Sue had agreed. She didn't want to come home and find their house burglarized again. Daddy said he should have put the lock on last night, but with the Stub Huggins adventure, he had forgotten about it. The lock did make Maggie feel better about going home.

The only pews open were the back two. The family slid into the front one of the two in case someone else happened to be running late. The girls tried to be quiet, but those hardwood floors seemed to magnify the sound every shoe click made.

They were already finished singing the hymns, and Pastor Olson paused to smile before he continued with his sermon. "God says, 'When thou vowest a vow unto God, defer not to pay it; for he hath no pleasure in fools: pay that which thou hast vowed. Better is it that thou shouldest not vow, than that thou shouldest vow and not pay.' We find that in the book of Ecclesiastes."

Maggie leaned her head back on the pew. Did God know her every thought? And did Pastor Olson read her mind? She had just been thinking of telling Daddy about Jed and Jess. Yesterday she had almost told Mrs. Valina her secret, and now Pastor Olson was preaching about keeping your promises. Mrs. Valina had said that a vow was the same as a promise. Maggie wondered if Pastor Olson thought they were the same.

Pastor Olson continued, "Today we don't use the word vow very much. It seems we prefer the word promise. Does the change of a word make the importance diminish? Sometimes I think that is how Satan plays with man's mind. Whether we say vow or promise, God's Word is still the same. It is better not to vow than to break a vow you have made. It is better not to promise than to make a promise and break it. It is the same difference. If you make it, don't break it. God's people should be known by their word. If a person knows everything that comes out of the mouths of God's people can be trusted, that person will start to see that God lives inside of His people. Don't misunderstand me. There are people without God in their hearts who feel strongly about keeping their word and many times bind it with a handshake. I want you to search your hearts. God's people should keep their word and be a testimony to those who do not have God in their hearts. Would those people want what you have if you don't keep your word?"

Maggie had to think about Pastor Olson's statement. It would mean keeping promises should be one way to know those people who have the God up in heaven in their hearts, and those who don't. That would also mean Maggie had to

keep her promise, so it would be another way that Jed could see she had the God up in heaven in her heart. Maggie bit her lip. Pastor Olson was right. Jed would keep his word with a handshake, but he didn't have the God up in heaven in his heart. She looked to the rafters. "Dear God in my heart, it looks like I have to leave it up to you for any help I might need because I made that promise to Jed, and I've got to keep it. Please, God, you have got to help me know what to do."

The door at the back of the church screeched open. Maggie twisted in her pew to see who had come in late. Mrs. Crenshaw drug Elbert in by one hand and gripped Cecil's arm in the other. Maggie caught Cecil's eye, and her heart squeezed. Cecil had a hopeless, defeated gaze, but Maggie thought he was trying to give her some message. Mr. Crenshaw followed Mrs. Crenshaw and the boys into the church, after apparently letting them off at the door so he could park the auto. Mrs. Crenshaw aimed Cecil into the pew first with Elbert following. They all squirmed into that last pew behind Maggie and her family.

Pastor Olson's voice was firm as he went on with his message. "Folks, we are in the midst of hard times. Our land is crying out for rain, and our souls are crying out to God for a rain of blessings. We must be faithful to Him so He can honor His people. I beg you not to be foolish in these times of drought on the land. Don't spread the drought to the soul. Some of you are not asking God what He wants you to do. You are trading your land, your bundles of blessing, all that God has given you for a handful of food with a promise to pay later. Folks, when later comes, you'll regret those promises. If you don't have the money now, you may not have it when it is due."

Maggie sure understood regretting promises. Yet how could she have helped Jed without that promise? Daddy and her new mama were good people. Surely they would have helped her. Martin and Mrs. Valina might have understood. In fact, Mrs. Valina had promised to give Maggie special medicine to help Jess.

Maggie felt the need to stretch. Kerwhap! She jumped as a songbook dropped on the floor. She must have bumped it when she stretched.

Opal gave her the evil eye because everyone turned to look at them again. Cecil reached down, picked it up, and handed it over the pew to Maggie. "Thanks," she mouthed.

As she held the hymnal in her hands, she noticed a piece of paper sticking out of the book. Maggie sat very still and glanced to either side. No one was watching. She opened the book to that page. The note had been folded to stick over the edge of the book. It said, "Meet me after church. VERY IMPORTANT!!!" Cecil must have already had the note written and had just been waiting for a chance to pass it to Maggie.

Maggie could feel herself beginning to sweat. How would she get a chance to meet Cecil? She looked down at the floor. It seemed her heart was sending a telegraph message with its pounding, "Please, dear God in my heart … "

With the final amen, Maggie stood. Mr. Crenshaw tapped Daddy on the arm, and they went out of the door together.

Cecil and Elbert scooted as fast as they could to get away from Mrs. Crenshaw. Mrs. Crenshaw waited until they were out of sight, then leaned over the pew and clutched Maggie's arm. "You don't have a job at my house anymore. You are not to step foot on my property ever again, you little brat!"

Sue reached out and grabbed Mrs. Crenshaw's hand and pulled it away from Maggie. Fire danced in Sue's eyes. "We have a few things to discuss. Maggie, take the girls outside and wait, please. Mrs. Crenshaw and I are going to have a little meeting of the minds at the altar."

Mrs. Crenshaw yanked her arm away from Sue. "I will go nowhere with the likes of you."

"Oh, yes, you will, because if you don't go to the altar with me right now, you will go to the sheriff with me, and I guarantee the sheriff will be on my side. It's your choice."

Maggie's mouth dropped. If she had thought Sue was mad last night, it had been nothing compared to today.

Pastor Olson stopped beside the two ladies. "Is there anything I can do to help the two of you?"

Sue glared at Mrs. Crenshaw. "That is up to Louise. Otherwise, we need just a few moments in private." Sue smiled at Pastor Olson.

Pastor Olson's eyes glinted. "Louise?" Maggie could tell Mrs. Crenshaw didn't like it a bit, but she nodded in agreement.

"Maggie, take the girls and follow Pastor Olson." Sue left no room for argument. Maggie took Opal's and Ruby's hands and followed Pastor Olson. "If you ever lay a hand on my daughter again, I will press charges … "

That was all Maggie heard as Pastor Olson shooed the girls quickly out and shut the church doors. Maggie felt a tug on her skirt. "Maggie," Cecil spoke in a low tone. "I got to talk to you."

Maggie jumped off the side of the steps. Quickly she looked to see if Opal and Ruby noticed. Opal was trying to listen at the door, and Ruby was pulling at her hand. Maggie took this opportunity to slip around the corner of the church with Cecil.

"Aunt Louise caught me last night trying to get Elbert out."

Maggie clutched her throat with her hand. "Are you okay?"

"I'm never going to be okay as long as I'm with Aunt Louise. I can't believe she and my mom are sisters. Aunt Louise is nothing like Mom."

"Cecil, I'm so sorry."

"She locks us in our rooms all the time. I know I can crawl out the window and jump to the ground, but Elbert can't. I ain't going to go off and leave Elbert with Aunt Louise." Cecil rubbed his neck.

"Tell Mr. Crenshaw. He can't know what your Aunt Louise is doing to you, or he wouldn't let it happen," Maggie pleaded.

Cecil shook his head. "That would just make her mad, and Uncle Arnold ain't there enough to stop her from doing it. She'd just wait until he left, then we'd really get a beatin'."

"Cecil, show him your leg. He'll believe you."

"No. Tomorrow when you come to work, get the key. She hangs it inside the pantry door. Then you can let us out of our rooms, and Elbert and I can sneak away."

"I can't. Your Aunt Louise just fired me. She said I couldn't come on your property again. Besides, I don't think my mama and daddy will let me come."

Cecil dropped his head against the wall of the church building. "What are we going to do?"

Maggie wiped the back of her hand across her forehead and leaned back against the weathered wood. "I don't know, Cecil, but the God up in heaven must have the answer, so pray."

Cecil's fists were knotted. "There's got to be some way."

Maggie had almost forgotten. "Cecil, what if you were able to stand your uncle's ladder under Elbert's window? Then after dark you two could sneak out of the house."

"It might work. It's worth a try." Cecil snapped his fingers. "Thanks, Maggie."

"And, Cecil … " Maggie touched his sleeve.

Cecil could feel the urgency in her voice. "What?"

"If you can find a way to get out, I have the perfect hiding place."

"Oh, there is going to be a way. There just has to be. Where is this hiding place?"

"In the basement of the Gatlin mansion."

"Gatlin mansion? It's all locked up. I should know. Aunt Louise has harped about it over and over."

"Yes, it's locked, but you could slide down the coal chute." Maggie grabbed his arm. "Listen, there is running water, food in the pantry, and beds, but the very best part is that your Aunt Louise would never think to look for you there. Besides, even if she did, she'd be locked out."

Cecil was nodding.

"You go ahead and crawl out your window tonight, and somehow I'll get away to come and help you get Elbert. Do we have a deal?"

"Deal."

Maggie and Cecil shook hands. Maggie felt a little nudge at the back of her mind. Was a deal like a promise? Should she have prayed about the deal first?

Mrs. Valina stepped around the corner. "Mmm. I thought I heard young voices around here. You both got people looking for you."

"Uh oh!" Cecil shot around the church and out of sight.

"Mmm. He don't look none too sick," Mrs. Valina raised her eyebrows.

Maggie smiled, "He's not, Mrs. Valina."

Mrs. Valina shook her head and sighed. "Missy, Missy, Missy. I ain't a-goin' to ask. Here's that medicine I done told you about last night. I thought I'd best bring it with me as it might be easier than you comin' by my house. I'm praying it will help."

"Thank you, Mrs. Valina. You are an angel." Maggie hugged her.

"I don't feel too much like an angel. I'm a-hopin' I'm doin' the right thing. Now your mama and daddy is a-waitin'."

Maggie backed a few steps then turned and flew to the front of the church. "Thank you!" she called one last time before she rounded the corner of the building.

Mrs. Valina shook her head. "That girl better be plenty prayed up. She's going to need it."

The Telegram

Something was wrong with Mr. Crenshaw. Maggie watched as his arms flew in different directions while he talked. Silently, Maggie came to stand beside him as he explained to Daddy, "I tell you, something is wrong with Louise. It has been ever since the guilty verdict on Thomas came in. She doesn't sleep at night. I don't think she eats. All she can talk about is 'Dodge City will be sorry they didn't stand behind their most upstanding citizen'—her cousin—Mr. Thomas Gatlin. She's talking nonsense. I can't make heads or tails of it. I am worried for her, but I'm more worried for Maggie. Please don't send her to work at our house until I have this all sorted out." Arnold Crenshaw ran his fingers over the top of his head.

Daddy nodded. "I appreciate your concern, Arnold, and I'll add my prayers to yours."

Sue slipped her hand through Sam's arm. "Is there anything we can do? I understand exactly what you are talking about. Louise doesn't seem herself. I just had a visit with her in church, and she threatened to have me arrested."

"I'm sorry, Sue. I won't let her try that." Mr. Crenshaw shook his head.

"Arnold, really, is there anything we can do?"

"It beats me. Pray. Maybe I can get it all figured out."

Maggie slipped her hand in Mr. Crenshaw's. "I can pray, too."

A wistful smile traveled over Mr. Crenshaw's face. "Maggie, I think I've learned about as much from you as I have from Pastor Olson."

Maggie studied Mr. Crenshaw. "You made a promise, too?"

Mr. Crenshaw burst into laughter. "Maggie, you never cease to cheer me. Pastor Olson did teach on promises, didn't he?"

"Yes, sir."

"Maggie, I promise you this: I will do everything in my power to get this cleared up, and you can come back to work. It may take a week or so, but with the Lord's help, we'll get it done."

"Thank you, Mr. Crenshaw."

"Let me help you, Maggie." Mr. Crenshaw lifted her into the back of the wagon.

On the way home, Opal leaned close to Maggie. "I saw you meeting Cecil around the side of the church. Do you like that horrid boy now?"

"Opal, he is not that horrid boy anymore. He's got the God up in heaven in his heart, and besides that, he helped me off the train and saved my life."

"Oh? Well, let me tell you what it looked like to me. It looked like you two were very serious. I think I should tell Mama," Opal threatened.

Ruby put her hand to her cheek and whispered to Maggie, "Opal's just jealous 'cause she thinks Cecil is cute."

"Opal?" Maggie raised her eyebrows.

"I do not," Opal said, but her cheeks turned beet red.

"You told me you thought he was cute," Ruby declared.

"I also told you not to tell anyone," Opal glared.

Maggie laughed. "So you do think he's cute." Opal plopped her hand over her mouth.

Maggie smiled. "Opal, he is cute, but he is not my beau. If you want to tell Mama, you go right ahead. Just think about it first, though. Mama will start asking questions, and before you know it, she'll have you figured out. Is that what you really want?"

"No." Opal crossed her arms.

"Good." Maggie realized now she was going to have Opal to worry about. That would definitely put her promise in danger.

Daddy had taken the long way home, and Maggie was relieved. She didn't want to go by the Gatlin mansion. She figured the less any of them saw it, the less thinking there would be about it.

Maggie was wondering about Jess when an auto eased up beside the wagon. It was Sheriff Ary, and he was motioning for Daddy to stop the horses.

"Whoa." Daddy tightened the reins.

Sheriff Ary left his engine running, got out of the car, and walked over to the wagon.

"What do you need, Sheriff? I know these horses of mine aren't breaking any speed limits," Daddy chuckled.

The sheriff laughed. "I like that sense of humor, Sam. It makes working with you a pleasure."

"You know the Lord says laughter is medicine for the soul."

"It sure is that," Sheriff Ary agreed.

Sam studied the sheriff, "What's on your mind? It must be something pretty important to be running me down on a Sunday."

Sheriff Ary nodded, then took a deep breath. "I just got a telegram. Seems late last night a man with a shotgun busted Thomas Gatlin out of the Larned State Hospital. So far they haven't found either of them."

"Sam," Sue gasped.

"How did that happen?" Daddy asked the question the rest of them wanted to ask.

"Well, the telegram was short, but from what I could gather, the man—probably Stub Huggins—walked right in the front doors after midnight. I guess someone didn't walk the rounds to make sure all was locked up tight. Anyway, the man strutted up to the front desk, leveled his shotgun on the lady, and she fainted dead away. Then he found the only guard on duty and ordered him to unlock Thomas Gatlin's room. The man didn't shoot the guard, but the knock he gave him on the head put the guard out for a couple of hours."

Silence followed. Maggie wondered if her troubles could get any worse.

"I'm sorry, Sam." Sheriff Ary shook his head. "I didn't want to worry you, but I thought you'd want to know."

"You're right. I want to know." Sam pressed his lips in a tight line.

"Now, between you and me, I don't think he'll head out this way." Sheriff Ary took off his hat and ran his finger over the sweatband inside the hat. "Dodge City is where everyone would expect him to go, and Thomas Gatlin is a smart man.

He's not going to want to be caught. I think he'll head any-where but here."

Sam rubbed his chin. "You may just be right. I hope you are, but just the same, I'll keep a look out for him."

"Good. I'll be looking for him, too. Now, I haven't told anyone else yet that Thomas Gatlin has escaped. I'm hoping that won't be necessary. I hope they catch him and lock him up before anyone from here finds out. I just pray Louise Cren-shaw doesn't get wind of it. I don't want that woman in my office again. I can't tell you how many times she's been in com-plaining over that guilty verdict. In fact, she stopped by my office after church and nearly got to my telegram before I could stop her. I had to stuff it into my pocket without reading it. I thought she would never leave."

"What in the world did Mrs. Crenshaw want from you on a Sunday?" Sam asked.

Sheriff Ary winked. "It seems that wife of yours attacked Mrs. Crenshaw in church after services."

"I most certainly did not," Sue denied.

"Sue? Am I going to have to arrest you?" Sheriff Ary chuckled.

"No, you are not," Sue dropped her mouth.

Sam laughed. "Why, Sheriff, ain't that your job?"

"Your wife? No problem. Now, taking care of Mrs. Cren-shaw, that should earn overtime," Sheriff Ary laughed.

Sue laid her hand on her husband's arm. "Sam, look." All eyes followed to where Sue was pointing. A black wall was tum-bling along the horizon.

"Not again, dear Lord. Not another dust storm," Sue's voice held desperation.

Sheriff Ary slapped his hat against his leg. "Looks like you folks had better head home, and I better get back to town. People will be going crazy."

"You're right, Sheriff. I'll be in tomorrow."

"See you." Sheriff Ary shoved his hat on his head, jumped into his auto, and revved up the engine.

"We've got time to get home before she hits." Sam tried to calm Sue while he flicked the reins to start up the horses. "Come on, Ben. Let's hurry it up, Maude."

Sue began giving orders. "Girls, when we get home, I want you to get out all the towels. Maggie, you help me get a couple of buckets of water. The last time one of these dirt storms hit, we ran out of water before the storm was over. We'll pour the water into the wash tub and cover it with a blanket to keep the dirt out. Sam, do you need any help with the horses?"

"If you can spare Maggie for a little bit, I'll have her help me with the horses while I go get Lulubelle. He glanced quickly at the sky. I think we've got enough time."

By now the girls were holding to the side of the wagon for dear life. Ben and Maude were running. As they came to their drive, Maggie closed her eyes and jumped from the slow, but still moving, wagon and swung open the gate. Maggie knew Daddy would scold her later, but there was no time now. He pulled the horses through and stopped. Maggie held her arms for Ruby to jump into them. They both tumbled, but Ruby had a soft landing. Sue yanked Ruby from Maggie so Maggie could climb aboard with Daddy to head for the barn.

"Don't ever do that again!" Daddy yelled as the first gust of wind hit.

At the shed, Daddy jumped down, turned, and swung Maggie to the ground. "Can you unhitch the team?" he yelled.

"Yes, sir."

Black dirt swirled about her skirt. Maggie felt the grit slip beneath her clothes.

"I'll be back as soon as I get Lulubelle," Daddy yelled. "When you have them tied to the manger, throw them some hay and head to the house. I'll be in as soon as I get Lulubelle taken care of."

Maggie seemed to be all thumbs. She needed to hurry, but the harder she tried, the more she tangled things.

Her hair lashed at her eyes. Eerie fingers of dust shifted through the slats of the shed, and Maggie thought she would remember that stormy, dusty smell forever. Finally, she had Ben and Maude tied to the manger. That was when she was supposed to go to the house, but it would help if she could put their feed sacks on their noses. She went to the feed bin, grabbed the sacks, and filled them halfway. Then she took them to the horses and slipped them over their heads. That would do two things. It would get them fed, and it would help filter the dust from their noses. Maggie patted Ben and Maude to comfort them. They were getting restless. The storm was whining now, and the air was dirty. Maggie tested the knots she had tied to make sure they would hold through the worst of it. She looked up to say a quick prayer before she headed to the house. "Dear God up …" Maggie caught her breath. There was a foot sticking over the stack of old boards in the rafters.

"She saw us!" He flung out of his mouth along with a string of words Maggie never used.

Maggie turned to run, but Stub Huggins dropped in front of her. "You ain't goin' nowhere, Girlie." Maggie drew back her leg and kicked as hard as she could.

"Eeow!" Stub grabbed his leg and began hopping.

Maggie backed away and slammed into arms that held her tight. She was relieved. "Daddy," she whispered.

Stub laughed. "Girlie, that ain't your daddy."

"Stub, shut up!" the voice of the man holding her growled.

Maggie gasped. That was another voice she knew. She recognized it from the trunk of a car in a gunnysack. It belonged to Mr. Thomas Gatlin.

"We got her now," Stub chuckled. "We done got her." Maggie screamed.

"You can holler all you want to, Girlie. Ain't nobody gonna hear you in this storm," Stub shoved his face closer.

Maggie tried to pull away, but the strong arms held her even tighter. She didn't call out again. She knew what Stub Huggins had said was true. No one could hear her over the moans of the wind, but somehow Maggie had to stall for time. Daddy would be back with Lulubelle any minute, and he would rescue her. How? It only took Maggie a second, and she decided. She would faint. Maggie rolled her eyes back and dropped as dead weight.

"Boss, she fainted dead away," Stub said in surprise. "I never figured that one to be a fainter. She's too feisty."

"She didn't faint. She must be expecting someone. We've got to get her out of here fast, or we'll have someone else that needs to be taken care of. Get the sack," Thomas Gatlin ordered.

"Not the sack!" Maggie yelled.

"Shut up, Girlie," Stub sneered.

Mr. Thomas Gatlin slapped his hand over her mouth, dragged her to the stack of firewood, and whopped Maggie over the head with a chunk of it. Maggie sank for real this time into dusty blackness.

Again

aggie rolled over and moaned. Her face was covered, but she wasn't trapped and tied inside the gunnysack. It was just thrown over the top of her. Memory hit hard. She was sure Mr. Thomas Gatlin and Stub Huggins were still around, but she hoped they hadn't heard her. She held very still, listening to the sounds. It didn't take long to figure out where she was. Maggie lay on the damp, dirt floor of the dugout where Jed had stashed Jess. She was tucked back where the floor met the roof of the dugout. Roots hung like crooked roads on a road map from the low, dirt ceiling, and they crawled out of the walls. The wind still cried as the dust blizzard blackened the opening of the cave along with the dry Kansas land.

Maggie's head throbbed, but she tried to ignore it. Finally, she spotted the two men huddled close to the opening of the cave. Both were just solid darker shapes in the midst of the dust blizzard. Both held handkerchiefs over their faces. Maggie strained to hear what the men were saying over the wailing wind. It was easy because the men were shouting so they could hear each other.

"Rats!" Stub Huggins slammed his fist into the palm of his hand. "Last time I was at that boxcar they didn't have a lock on the door. Rats! We could have been chowin' down now, and I'm plenty hungry. I could eat a horse. It's been a couple of long days. It feels like my innards are tryin' to eat their own selves."

"Shut up, Huggins." Thomas Gatlin looked out through the opening of the dark hole.

"You think the girlie is dead this time?"

"I hope so. If she lives to talk, we aren't going to see the light of day for a very long time. Fact is, they will probably execute the both of us," Thomas Gatlin said.

Stub swallowed and rubbed his neck.

Maggie didn't think Mr. Thomas Gatlin sounded like a crazy man, but he sure had acted like one in the courtroom the day he was found guilty. Maybe he had a split personality.

Stub giggled and dropped his hand from his neck. "They ain't found me the first time, and I reckon I ain't goin' to let 'em find me this time. All I want is that money you said you had stashed away. It'll take me a far piece away from here and set me up real good."

"Huggins, I said you'll get your money."

"Well, I'm not a trustin' man. Until I get my money, this here scattergun and me are goin' to be on you like a duck on a June bug." Stub patted his shotgun.

"Stub Huggins, you try using that gun on me, and I promise you I'll kill you." Thomas said that so matter-of-factly that Maggie felt a chill. He made it sound like it was an everyday thing, like getting up in the morning and putting on your clothes. Maggie's mind spun. Maybe he had killed before. Maybe he was crazy in such a way that he thought whatever he wanted to do was right just because he wanted to do it. Mr. Thomas Gatlin reminded Maggie of the raging dust storm. It was darkly sinister and destructive, yet when it settled down, the peace was as calm as deep water … deep, menacing water. Fingers of panic crawled up Maggie's throat and began to choke her. "Dear God up in heaven, you have just got to help me," Maggie prayed silently.

Through the dusty darkness, she watched Stub, and she could tell he was spooked, too. Stub spit, and Maggie remembered how he had spit a stream of slimy tobacco juice at Mr. Crenshaw's feet. Stub was silent for a while, but Maggie could feel his need to keep talking. She hoped he did. She hated the howl of the storm and the thick, dusty air, but they also helped to keep the men's attention away from her. Maggie licked her cracked lips. They tasted of dirt.

"What are you going to do?" Stub asked Thomas Gatlin.

"Well, I am not going to stay around this town. Dodge City turned its back on me. It doesn't deserve me. I just hate that I can't ruin the city before I go." He had been fiddling with a stick and had snapped it in two. He suppressed a low growl from within. "I owned over half of this town. I have the IOUs. All of them are signed and locked in the safe in my basement, and I can't do a thing with them." He tossed the sticks into the storm and watched the wild wind suck them up and sweep them away.

"That where your money is, too?" Stub asked.

Thomas Gatlin laughed. "Now that would be too easy, Stub, wouldn't it? No. You still need me, Huggins." Stub chuckled nervously.

Thomas Gatlin stretched. "As soon as this storm is over, we've got two stops. I'm going to check on my place, and I'm going to see Louise. That's where we'll be headed."

"What about the girlie?" Stub motioned over his shoulder with his head.

"We have been in here over twenty-four hours. She hasn't moved. She's dead, Huggins. Dead."

"What if someone finds her?"

"Huggins, by the time she's found, I'm going to be long gone. If you want to stick around, Stub, go ahead."

"I'm only stickin' around 'til I got that money in my hands and find my boys. Rats! I bet that girlie knew where my boys were." Stub was fidgety. He stood up and leaned against the sod wall. Maggie hoped he didn't mosey over her way. He did.

Maggie held her breath and closed her eyes. She felt Stub walk over and gaze down at her. He kicked her in the side. Maggie swallowed a sob and refused to move. She knew he waited to see if she was alive. When he was satisfied she was dead, he moved back to the mouth of the dugout and slid down the dirt wall across from Thomas Gatlin. "Maybe we should cave in this dugout when we leave. That a way ain't no one gonna find that girlie."

Maggie tried not to gasp. That would mean she would be buried alive. Her heart began pounding overtime, and for once, she was glad of the rumbling wind.

"Huggins, if you want to take time to try to cave in this dugout, you go right ahead. I am not waiting around."

"You'd like that wouldn't you, Gatlin? You'd like me to stay behind. Well, it ain't gonna happen. You ain't gettin'

outta my sight," Stub growled. Maggie felt relief rush through her whole body.

Thomas Gatlin laughed. When his laughter died, the men just stared across the cave at each other. Maggie could tell neither trusted the other. Both men were tense, and since they both had been awake all the while the storm had thrown its temper tantrum, it wouldn't be long before one of them snapped.

Hours later, the wind ran out of rage and began to merely whimper. Dust settled, and the silence was breathtaking.

Thomas Gatlin stood. "Well, Huggins, I'm going. You can tag along, or you can cave in the dugout. It's up to you. I don't care." Stub scrambled to his feet.

To Maggie's relief, both men stepped out of the dugout without a single glance backward. Maggie dared not move. She wanted to make sure they were gone. Then there were two things she had to do. She had to keep Cecil and Elbert from going to the Gatlin mansion, and she had to get Jed and Jess out of it. Maggie didn't know which to do first. Logic told her Jed and Jess might be in trouble if they were found, but Stub was their pa, and surely their pa would keep them safe. Cecil and Elbert wouldn't be so lucky.

Maggie's legs tingled like fireworks on the Fourth of July. She had to dance a bit before she could trust them to work. Quietly she edged to the mouth of the cave. It was dark outside, but even that darkness was lighter than the depths of the dugout.

Maggie watched as Thomas Gatlin and Stub Huggins disappeared into the cottonwoods along the Arkansas River. Maggie decided to go the opposite direction. Steadily she walked toward the Crenshaw house. Her legs wobbled for only a little way, and finally Maggie broke into a trot that made her head pound. Never had the Crenshaw house seemed so far away.

Maggie was gasping for air when she turned into the tree-lined lane. A light shone in the sitting room, but there was no way Maggie was going to knock on the door. She needed to know who was in there and what was going on. If she could catch Cecil or Elbert's eye, she could motion for them to meet her outside somehow.

Like a shadow, Maggie blended with the side of the house and dropped beneath the window. She had to know what was going on in there.

"Louise, just how long have they been gone?" Maggie heard Mr. Crenshaw slam his fist onto the table.

Louise stood. "I don't have to listen to this."

Maggie peeked into the window. She saw Mr. Crenshaw stand and take Louise by the shoulders. "Louise, what has happened to you? When we met, I thought you were the most beautiful thing that walked the face of the earth. Now I don't even know you."

"You are right. You don't know me."

"I don't understand, though. I don't understand how you can be so beautiful on the outside and so cold and hard and empty on the inside. You are not what I thought at all," Mr. Crenshaw searched her face.

"And just what would you have me to be?"

Maggie continued watching as Mr. Crenshaw dropped his hands and paced about the room. "I would have you be as beautiful on the inside as you are on the outside. I want that sweet, gentle spirit ..." he waved his hands in the air, "a spirit like Maggie Daniels!"

"That little brat!" Louise fumed.

"That little girl is the picture of God's pure love. I have never heard her say one bad word to anyone in all the time I have known her. She has been warmth to this cold house. She has been laughter and love and honesty. She has been the perfect example for all of us." Mr. Crenshaw looked up at nothing. He stuck his hands in his pockets and slid his fingers through his change. He pulled out a quarter. "See this, Louise? Maggie treasured the smallest things. I don't know if you treasure anything."

"You are wrong, Arnold. Thomas Gatlin is important to me. This house is important to me. Prestige is important to me," Louise seethed.

"And me, Louise? Am I? Was I ever important to you?" Mr. Crenshaw looked beaten.

Maggie saw Mrs. Crenshaw look at the floor. "Don't be silly, Arnold. Of course, you are important to me. Why, you are the bank president."

"The bank president? That is all I am to you? Louise, I think Maggie was right. I don't think you have ever planted that mustard seed God offers. I don't even know if you would recognize a mustard seed."

"Arnold, what has a mustard seed got to do with anything?" Maggie saw Mrs. Crenshaw look at him as if she thought he was crazy.

Mr. Crenshaw took a deep breath. "I guess nothing, Louise." Mr. Crenshaw walked around the room, his shoulders drooping. Maggie watched him as he stopped in front of his wife. "Just tell me where you think the boys might be."

"I told you I don't know. You weren't here when the storm started. I sent them to their rooms and told them to stay there.

When I called, they didn't come. When I went to get them, they were gone, but the storm had already started, and I had a million things to do to keep the dust out. That is all I know." Maggie noticed Mrs. Crenshaw just shrugged her shoulders.

For a long moment, Mr. Crenshaw stared at Mrs. Crenshaw. Finally, he shook his head, "Louise, I'm going out to look for those boys. I better find them, and they better be okay." He pointed his finger as if he wanted to say more, but he dropped his hand. He crossed to the door, and Maggie heard it slam.

This was Maggie's chance. She flew around the side of the house and slid to a stop in front of Mr. Crenshaw. At what point the tears had started streaming down her face she didn't know.

"Maggie!" Mr. Crenshaw dropped to his knees and opened his arms wide.

Maggie dove into them. "Mr. Crenshaw, I think I know where Cecil and Elbert went."

Trembling, Mr. Crenshaw asked, "You do? Are they all right?"

Maggie nodded. "I hope so. Do you have a gun?"

CHAPTER 14

A Gun

"A gun?"

Maggie nodded. "I think Cecil and Elbert went to the Gatlin mansion, and I know for certain Mr. Thomas Gatlin and Stub Huggins are headed that way … if they aren't already there."

Mr. Crenshaw took a deep breath and rubbed his hand over his eyes. "Sheriff Ary told me Thomas had escaped, but I had hoped he wouldn't come here. I certainly pray Louise doesn't find out."

Mr. Crenshaw didn't bother to say any more. "I'll get my gun, and we'll take the Model T." Mr. Crenshaw ran to the house and burst through the door. In seconds he dashed out toward the garage, all the while shoving his .38 Special in the waistband of his trousers.

Mrs. Crenshaw followed. "Just what are you going to do with that gun?" she demanded.

Maggie ran after Mr. Crenshaw, but Mrs. Crenshaw was faster than Maggie would have believed. Mrs. Crenshaw dug her fingers into Maggie's arm and yanked her around. "What are you doing here? Get off this property at once!" she shook Maggie.

"Louise, let her go!" Mr. Crenshaw yelled. "She is with me." Mr. Crenshaw backed up the Model T, leaned over, and threw the door open.

Mrs. Crenshaw's eyes danced between the two. "So that is the way it is?" She didn't wait for an answer. "Then I'm coming with you, too." The angry woman stepped to the door of the auto, but Maggie slipped in before she could. That didn't stop Mrs. Crenshaw. She frowned, shoved in beside Maggie, and slammed the door shut.

Mr. Crenshaw asked Maggie, "Now how do you know Thomas is at the Gatlin mansion?"

Mrs. Crenshaw burst into the conversation. "Thomas is here?"

"Louise, we don't have time for you to interrupt. Maggie, how do you know?" Mrs. Crenshaw glowered beside Maggie, but she kept quiet.

"He and Stub Huggins got a hold of me when the dust blizzard started. We were all in that old dugout along the railroad tracks all through the storm. They thought I was dead, so I was able to listen to them talk."

"Maggie, does your daddy and mama know you are okay?" Mr. Crenshaw asked.

Maggie shook her head. "Mr. Thomas Gatlin and Stub Huggins didn't give me a chance to go tell them before they took me."

"Are you sure you are up to going with me? Maybe we should take you home first, so your mama and daddy won't have further worry." Mr. Crenshaw slid a glance at Maggie as he slowed to turn from his drive.

Maggie shook her head. "Honest, we have to keep Cecil and Elbert from hiding in the Gatlin mansion if they are not already there. I'm afraid of what might happen to them."

"Maggie, we have got to let your mama and daddy know you are okay." Mr. Crenshaw started to set the brakes, so he could turn the Model T around.

"No." Maggie twisted her hands together. "Mr. Thomas Gatlin and Stub Huggins will kill Cecil and Elbert."

Mrs. Crenshaw laughed. "You have got to be making this story up. In the first place, Thomas is in Larned State Hospital."

"No, he is not. Sheriff Ary told us he escaped the night before the storm hit. The sheriff wanted us to know. Then when I was in the shed tying the horses, I saw Mr. Gatlin and Stub hiding in the rafters above me. Mr. Gatlin hit me with a chunk of firewood, and they carted me away with them."

"That is a bunch of malarkey," Mrs. Crenshaw hissed.

"It is not. Look at this." Maggie pulled her hair to the side where a purple lump protruded from her head.

Mrs. Crenshaw shoved her face closer to Maggie's. "If Thomas hit you, I guarantee that you deserved it."

"Louise, that's enough. Either keep quiet or get out of the auto." Mr. Crenshaw stopped at the Gatlin gate and began pounding on the horn.

They watched as a light came on inside Valina and Martin's house. Martin opened the door and looked out. Mr. Crenshaw jumped out of the Model T, left the door gaping, and ran over to Martin. "Martin, we need to get into the mansion, and I need you to drive my auto to get the sheriff."

Valina had crowded to the door behind Martin. "The sheriff? What's wrong, Mr. Crenshaw?"

"I've got Maggie, and she says the boys are in trouble. I need the sheriff."

"Missy Maggie? I declare! That young'un's folks been lookin' all over for her. They need to be told." Valina shoved past and headed for the car.

Mr. Crenshaw clapped his hands with an idea. "You are right. Listen, Valina, how about you driving to get Sheriff Ary?" Then he turned to Martin. "How about you cutting across the pasture to let the Daniels family know Maggie is safe and with me?"

Valina threw her hands up in the air. "You mean you're going to have me drive that monster?"

Martin chuckled. "I'm cutting across the pasture for sure. I guarantee I want to be out of her way, and I'm hoping the pasture is far enough out of her way."

"Martin, you ought to be ashamed of yourself," Valina shook her finger. "Why, with the good Lord beside me, I can do anything. The Lord done told me that in His Good Book where it says, 'I can do all things through Christ which strengtheneth me.' Martin, I am going to master this fine machine, and you had best stay out of my way while I do."

Martin nodded. "I believe I'll do just that." Valina's husband chuckled as he turned to Mr. Crenshaw. "I think you created a monster, letting her drive your auto, but it's your Model T."

Valina headed toward the car with a stubborn will.

Maggie dove from the vehicle and ran to Mrs. Valina.

"You okay, Missy?"

Maggie fell into Mrs. Valina's arms, and she was sure the God in heaven sent those arms to take His place.

"Missy, you is an answer to prayer for sure, a sight for sore eyes. Are you coming with me?" Mrs. Valina asked.

Maggie stepped away from the warmest place she knew. "No, ma'am. I have to show Mr. Crenshaw where Cecil and Elbert and Jed and Jess are. I have to, because they are in a heap of trouble."

With venom, Mrs. Crenshaw glared at Mrs. Valina and hissed, "You will not drive this car. I don't even want the likes of you to touch it."

Mrs. Valina smiled. "Mrs. Crenshaw, this is important business. Your man done told me to drive this here car to get help. Now if you want to ride along, you're most welcome. If you don't, then you'd best be unloading yourself because I'm fixing to drive." With that Valina pulled herself into the Model T and settled behind the steering wheel as the motor puttered.

"Arnold Jack Crenshaw! Get this woman out of this vehicle," Mrs. Crenshaw ordered. Mrs. Valina revved the engine. Mrs. Crenshaw didn't wait for Arnold's answer. She plunged out of the auto headfirst, somersaulted, and lay sprawled unladylike on the hard, dry ground.

By now Martin had the gate wide open. Mrs. Valina had no idea where reverse was, so she threw the car in gear and sailed through the gate, throwing a cloud of dirt everywhere. She spun a circle in the Gatlin yard to turn back toward town, stepped on the gas, and swerved through the gate again flying down the road.

Everyone heard her yell, "Bless my soul, this auto can fly!"

Martin called after her, "Open your eyes, Woman!"

As the car raced past the gate and the dust settled, Maggie gasped. Mrs. Crenshaw's dress flapped over her head as she dashed from in front of the speeding auto. She rolled, tumbled, scooted, and plunged into a crawl on all fours to get out of the path of the wild vehicle.

In the quiet that settled after the auto disappeared in a cloud of dust, everyone gathered together. All eyes settled on Mrs. Crenshaw, but no one said a word. Then she broke the silence. "Arnold Jack, get over here and help me up."

Mr. Crenshaw strode over and pulled Mrs. Crenshaw to her feet. Without a word to his wife, he turned to Martin. "You do have a key to the mansion, don't you?"

"Yes, sir. I'll go get it afore I head to the Daniels' place."

Maggie tugged at Mr. Crenshaw's sleeve. "I know a way to get inside the mansion without a key."

Mrs. Crenshaw pointed her finger at Maggie. "I told you that girl was no good, getting into places with no keys. That's called breaking and entering." Mrs. Crenshaw tapped her foot.

"Louise, that's enough." Mr. Crenshaw stepped between her and Maggie.

Martin handed the keys to Mr. Crenshaw. "If you don't need me, I'll go on to the Daniels' place."

"Thank you, Martin."

Martin scurried off. The other three turned toward the house.

Maggie whispered, "Mr. Crenshaw, please let me go in my secret way. I want to warn the boys—that is, if they are there."

"I don't know. Why don't we ease up to the mansion and listen a bit. That way we'll know if Thomas and Stub are even around." Maggie nodded.

Mrs. Crenshaw stood with her arms crossed. "Ridiculous," she spat.

Mr. Crenshaw turned to Louise. "Then you just stay where you are, Louise. Come on, Maggie." Both crept up the stairs. Both crossed the porch, and both leaned against the door to listen. Nothing.

Mrs. Crenshaw tramped after them. "Just knock on the door," Mrs. Crenshaw advised, although she was wise enough to do it in a whisper.

Carefully Mr. Crenshaw slid the key in the lock and turned. The well-oiled door eased open, and the darkness of the mansion poured onto the moonlit porch. The foreboding door gaped wide. Everyone stood still, not wanting to step into that patch of velvety darkness. Maggie was sure she could hear her own heart beating, but that was all she heard.

Mrs. Crenshaw tromped up the steps and across the porch. "This is utterly ridiculous." She stomped past them and stepped over the threshold, and Maggie held her breath. A long, quiet second passed. It seemed like the whole world had stopped breathing. Then Mrs. Crenshaw screamed. Maggie shook and flattened her body against the outside wall of the mansion.

"Thomas!" Slowly Mrs. Crenshaw backed out the door with a shotgun barrel against her chest. Mrs. Crenshaw threw herself into Mr. Crenshaw's arms.

Mr. Thomas Gatlin appeared. He held the shotgun and drew a bead on Mr. Crenshaw. "Well, isn't this nice. This is better than I had planned. I didn't even have to send for Louise and her banker husband. Come on in, Arnold. Bring Louise with you. We have some talking to do. Let's just gather around my dining table. Stub," he called over his shoulder, "light us a lamp and set it on the dining room table."

Mr. Crenshaw helped Mrs. Crenshaw to stand on her own, and from behind her he motioned for Maggie to hide around the corner of the porch.

Maggie slid out of sight. She hadn't been seen yet, and she didn't want to be seen. Maggie stepped around the corner and slinked like a cat to the edge of the dining room window. The lamp had already been set on the table, but she couldn't see Stub Huggins anywhere, and that could be dangerous. She would have to listen for him.

Mr. Thomas Gatlin made Mr. Crenshaw sit at the end of the table while he sat on the other end opposite his hostage. Mr. Crenshaw's back was to the window, and Maggie wished it were the other way around. She hated having Mr. Thomas Gatlin facing the window. He might see her. Thomas Gatlin rested the shotgun on the table, aimed at Mr. Crenshaw's belly. "Arnold, have you ever seen anyone gut-shot before? It isn't a pretty sight, so you two listen very carefully to what I want you to do."

Mr. Crenshaw didn't make a sound. Mrs. Crenshaw did, however. "Thomas, this is not necessary."

"Louise, sit down beside your husband and don't talk. The world will be a better place."

Mrs. Crenshaw gaped. "Thomas, I am on your side."

"Really? Did you get that kid of your sister's to tell the lawyers he was lying?"

"Not yet, but I will."

"Louise?" Mr. Crenshaw started.

Thomas Gatlin cocked the gun. "Louise, I told you to get that done."

Louise squirmed a bit. "Thomas, you know I will. I have always done whatever you have asked me to do."

Mr. Crenshaw studied his wife. "Louise, just what have you done?"

Thomas Gatlin laughed. "Louise, go ahead and tell him." Oddly enough, she only looked at the floor.

"What's the matter, Louise? Don't you want him to know? Let me help you," Thomas laughed again.

"Please, Thomas. You promised that no one would ever have to know," Louise begged. From outside the window, Maggie almost felt sorry for her.

"Louise, you shouldn't keep secrets from your husband. Tell him why you married him."

Mrs. Crenshaw rested her hand on the back of the chair and dropped her gaze to the floor.

Thomas Gatlin continued. "I told her to marry you, Arnold. I told her to marry you because you were the bank president, and I thought I could use you someday. Today just happens to be the day. You are going to take me to the bank, and we are going to make one huge withdrawal. I am going to take all of Dodge City's money. That will serve those good citizens right."

Mr. Crenshaw studied the top of the table for a long moment before he answered, "No, Thomas. You cannot make me do that."

"Really? Then let me tell you what else Louise has done for me."

Mrs. Crenshaw dropped to the floor on her knees and pleaded, "Please, Thomas!"

Thomas Gatlin didn't even bother to look at Louise. "My devoted cousin here helped my wife in her last days. Do you want to tell Arnold how you helped, Louise?" Mrs. Crenshaw shook her head wildly.

Thomas didn't care. "She held a pillow over my dear wife's head."

"I did not hold the pillow, Thomas! I walked in on you when you were holding it."

Compassion welled up in Maggie's heart for Mrs. Crenshaw as she began to sob.

Thomas Gatlin shrugged. "But, Louise, you never told anyone, either. That is the same as holding the pillow. Besides, who will Dodge City believe? You or me?" Louise dropped her head.

Mr. Crenshaw was in shock, "Why, Louise? Why?"

Thomas Gatlin chuckled. "You see, I needed to marry Sue to keep the Gatlin estate in the family, but I couldn't very well do that with a wife, could I? Besides, my wife was going to divorce me and tell everything she knew. I couldn't have that happen." By now Mrs. Crenshaw had crumbled at Mr. Gatlin's side, bawling.

"And that's not all. Louise, tell Arnold about Sue's husband, her first husband." Thomas was enjoying himself.

Louise wailed over and over, "No … No … No … "

Thomas giggled, and Maggie thought he was crazy. "She's the one that drove by and threw a cigarette in the gasoline Sue's husband was standing in."

"That is not true!" Louise shouted. "You threw that cigarette across the car to me. I caught it. It burned me, and I threw it out the window. It landed in the puddle of gasoline. It was an accident!"

Maggie couldn't see Mr. Crenshaw's face, but if he felt anything like she did, it had to be drained of all color. Maggie only felt pity and a little sick at her stomach for Mrs. Crenshaw.

Thomas continued, "You see, Arnold, if you don't help me, your lovely wife will spend the rest of her life in jail."

Silence settled until Mr. Crenshaw spoke, "Louise, I'm sorry for all you've been through. I want to help you."

Mrs. Crenshaw broke into a sob. "You can't help me, Arnold. No one can help me. Everyone will believe Thomas and not me. The things I have done and have kept secret are too horrible for anyone to be able to help me."

Mr. Crenshaw didn't give up. "Louise, God can help you. Remember Maggie? Remember Maggie's mustard seed?"

Thomas slapped his hand down on the table. "Shut up. We're going to head for the bank, and you are going to get the money for me."

Stub Huggins burst through the door. "Boss, someone is out there. I heard something!"

"Well, go see who it is, Huggins, and take care of him."

When Maggie heard Stub throw the front door open, she ran. She ran to the back of the house, dove, and swooped down the coal chute.

CHAPTER 15

Maggie's Mustard Seed

M aggie skidded on her belly down the chute and landed on a pile of coal. Pain burst through her body, but she didn't dare yell. She had made enough noise as she slid to the bottom, and she didn't want to draw more attention to herself. She lay very still and listened to the deafening quiet in the chocolate black darkness.

Maggie heard the flap of the coal chute screech open. "I got you now, whoever you are. Your hide belongs to me. I heard you drop down this here chute." It was Stub Huggins. Maggie couldn't see him, but she sure recognized that voice.

Stub Huggins chucked a hunk of coal down the chute and laughed as he heard the dull thud hit his target. "I'm a comin' for you." Maggie felt cold chills run through her bruised body as she heard the flap to the chute slam shut.

Maggie quickly tumbled off the pile of coal and let her eyes get used to the basement's darkness. She was glad the window wells let in a bit of moonlight. She listened, but she couldn't hear a sound. "Jed?" she called softly, hoping the boys were down here.

No one answered. Maybe they weren't there, or maybe they were too afraid to answer. She called one more time, "Jed? Cecil? Elbert? Jess? It's me, Maggie." Still no one answered.

Maybe they were in another part of the house. She shuddered. If that were true, it meant Maggie was alone in the basement with Stub Huggins headed her way, and this basement was a death trap. Maggie fumbled through the shadowy darkness for a weapon and a place to hide. The only thing she could see was the ghostly glow of one of Mr. Gatlin's bowling pins from his bowling alley. Maggie grabbed it and tiptoed to the stairs. Maybe she could hide beneath the stairs until Stub came down them. Then while he was snooping around the basement looking for her, she could run up the stairs and get away. It seemed like a slim chance, but it was the only thing she could think to do.

Maggie hunched low beneath the stairwell. Her shoes sank into the damp softness of moist dirt. Dirt? Maggie thought the basement had a stone floor. Maggie twisted around and felt a hole where a big brick had been pried loose from the side of the wall. A sliver of moonlight revealed a rusted box lying open on the floor. Maggie set the bowling pin down and sifted her fingers through the dirt. She found what looked like a gold coin, wrapped her fist around it, and pushed it deep into her pocket. Was this a piece of the money Thomas Gatlin had promised Stub? If Stub already had his money, why was he still hanging around? Maybe Stub's job was not done yet. Maggie gasped softly as the door at the top of the basement stairs cracked open.

"Whoever you are, you can be sure this is the only way out, so you might as well show your own self. Don't be making me come down there after your no good hide."

The only move Maggie dared make was to pick up the bowling pin and grasp it tightly in her hands. The sound of Stub Huggins's voice seemed to make her heart pound, "Please, God. Please, God. Please, God," with each beat.

"Whoever you is, you is just stallin', and that only makes me more riled up." Stub opened the door wide. A shaft of light streamed down into the dark basement. Stub must have switched on the gas lights outside the entry to the basement door.

Maggie looked up through the open slats of the basement steps. Stub's figure loomed bigger than life as he stood on the top step as if ready to pounce. Her eyes widened. If Stub were to look down, he could see her through the open steps. Slowly she looked away, fearful she might attract his attention just because she was staring at him.

Maggie heard the next step creak. Stub was coming down. She had to keep her eyes on him now so she would know when to make a run for it.

"Ain't no place you can hide yourself from ole Stub." Stub half sang the words as if they were part of a simple nursery rhyme. Over and over he chanted: "Ain't no place you can hide. Ain't no place you can hide."

Chills crawled up Maggie's neck. Maybe Stub was crazy, too.

Stub stepped off the last step and moved to the center of the basement. Slowly he turned in one direction and then another, his eyes searching the walls and peering into every corner.

Maggie stifled a gasp as she got a clear view of Stub. He held a mining pick in his hands, and Maggie knew he meant to kill her with it.

Now Stub's back was turned. This was the only chance she was likely to get, and she had to take it. Maggie grabbed the bowling pin tightly, crept from beneath the stairs, and streaked around. She was halfway up the steps when Stub grabbed at her. His hand slipped across the hem of her dress, and it swept passed his grasp. Maggie shrieked in horror.

When he got a good look at her, Stub's face drained, and his eyes bulged. Maggie Daniels was the last person he expected to see here. She was supposed to have been dead in the old dugout. That's where he had left her. "Eeow! You're dead!" He yelled. "A ghost! You've got to be a ghost!" Stub threw the mining pick into the basement darkness and sailed past Maggie, up the stairs, and through the door, all the while screeching and screaming.

Maggie sank onto the step hugging the bowling pin. Her heart was pounding faster than ever. Maggie knew she had to get out of the basement. She jumped and rushed up the remaining stairs. Staying within the shadows of the hallway on the floor above the basement, she leaned against the wall, trembling. She heard Stub as he shot out the front door and went screaming into the night.

"God have mercy. What was that?" Mr. Crenshaw asked.

Thomas Gatlin laughed. "I would say Stub must have found something scrounging around in the dark. Sounds as if Stub took care of the problem."

Maggie felt a sense of triumph as she overheard what Thomas Gatlin had just said. "Maybe instead of Stub doing the 'taking care,' someone like the God in my heart took care of Stub," she thought. "Why else would Stub believe I was a ghost?" Maggie set the bowling pin against the wall and inched closer to the dining room doorway. Thomas Gatlin was still sitting at the table, his back turned to Maggie.

"Now let's get back down to business," Gatlin commanded. "Louise, get off the floor and have a seat. I'm sure Arnold will come around to my way of thinking. If he doesn't, he will be visiting you in prison. We're talking murder, you know, and that means the gallows!"

Maggie had to calm her breathing as she kept her eyes on Thomas Gatlin's back from the dining room doorway.

He offered an evil chuckle. "Arnold, you know they will let you watch, if you tell them you'd like to witness your wife's hanging." From across the table, Mr. Crenshaw started in anger toward Gatlin's shotgun.

"I wouldn't even think of it, Arnold, my friend." Mr. Gatlin coldly stroked the trigger with his finger. He glanced at his cousin. "Louise, get up off the floor. You make me ill." Mr. Crenshaw started to stand to help his wife.

Thomas Gatlin smiled. "Louise can get up by herself. You stay put." He tapped his finger on the table. "Now, Louise, get up off the floor."

Somehow Maggie had to help. She looked at the bowling pin she had placed by the wall. Her eyes shifted about. It was the bowling pin or nothing. Yet, what was that against Thomas Gatlin's gun?

Maggie watched Mrs. Crenshaw slowly lift herself from the floor. She was sobbing uncontrollably, yet at the same time acted like a trained animal obeying its master. Then Mrs. Crenshaw caught sight of Maggie in the shadows behind Thomas Gatlin. As recognition hit, Mrs. Crenshaw wiped her eyes. "Maggie?" she said hoarsely.

Thomas Gatlin yanked his head around with a surprised glare. His mouth dropped, "You're supposed to be dead!"

Instantly, Mr. Crenshaw surged to his feet and dove for the shotgun. Maggie watched as Mr. Thomas Gatlin swiped the shotgun from beneath Mr. Crenshaw's fingers and pointed it directly at him.

Mrs. Crenshaw yelled, "Not this time, you don't!" She jumped in front of the barrel just as Thomas pulled the trigger.

Mrs. Crenshaw twisted and was thrown to the floor. Mr. Crenshaw fell beside her. He gently pulled her into his arms, crooning her name over and over again. "Louise … Louise …"

Maggie couldn't see where the blood was coming from, but it spread everywhere on both Mr. and Mrs. Crenshaw.

Mrs. Crenshaw gasped through shallow gulps. "Lord, God, forgive me." She turned pleading eyes to Mr. Crenshaw, "Forgive me, Arnold. Please, forgive me."

"Louise, it'll be okay. You've just got to hang on," Mr. Crenshaw rocked her and gently sobbed. As he cradled his wife and looked into her eyes, he never thought to look at her wound.

Louise grabbed her husband's collar and pleaded once again, "Forgive me!"

Mr. Crenshaw nodded lovingly.

Then Maggie saw the most amazing thing. She saw Mrs. Crenshaw smile for the first time ever. Mr. Crenshaw had been right. His wife was a beautiful person.

"Arnold," Mrs. Crenshaw began weakly, "I got Maggie's mustard seed." Mrs. Crenshaw let go of her husband's collar and slumped from his hold.

"Louise? Louise?" Mr. Crenshaw groaned as he buried his head in his wife's limp body.

Thomas Gatlin held the gun against his leg and coldly stroked his cheek. "Arnold, let her be. She's better off dead. We still have business to discuss."

Maggie was sobbing because the only dead person she had ever seen before was her mama. She didn't even have to close her eyes to remember Daddy wading out of the pond carrying Mama's lifeless body. The memory still stabbed through her whole being. Maggie knew exactly how Mr. Crenshaw felt. Slowly she stepped from behind Thomas Gatlin and moved to Mr. Crenshaw's side. She held tightly to her weapon with one hand while she laid her other hand on his shoulder. In a flash she was torn away by Mr. Thomas Gatlin as he wildly swung her into his clutches and jabbed Mr. Crenshaw with his shotgun.

Slowly Mr. Crenshaw looked up. Like a fragile, precious possession, Mr. Crenshaw placed his wife on the floor. He didn't take time to wipe his eyes. He stood to his feet in one fluid motion. Maggie thought he looked stronger and taller than ever before as he faced Thomas Gatlin.

Thomas Gatlin smirked. "If you wouldn't go to the bank to save Louise, maybe you'll go to the bank for this." Raging anger gave Gatlin the extra strength to dangle Maggie with one arm and aim the shotgun with the other.

"Thomas, if you hurt her, I will kill you," Mr. Crenshaw spoke with quiet determination.

"Then you had best come with me to the bank, Arnold."

"Put her down, and I'll go." Mr. Crenshaw's eyes never left Gatlin's piercing, threatening stare.

"Not a chance. She comes with us."

For the first time Maggie realized Mr. Gatlin had been in such a frenzy he had not noticed the bowling pin she still gripped in her hand. This was her chance. She grasped the neck of the pin with both hands and with all the strength she could muster, she swung the pin, smacking Thomas Gatlin in the face.

His double barrel shotgun blasted a shot through the ceiling. He threw Maggie and fell to the floor.

That was the distraction Mr. Crenshaw needed. He yanked his .38 Special from where it had been hidden in the back waistband of his trousers covered by his suit coat and aimed.

Maggie watched as Mr. Thomas Gatlin groaned and rolled over on his back. Blood poured from his smashed nose, and his lip was split wide open. The pin had slid across the floor and was still spinning in a circle. Maggie scrambled to Mr. Crenshaw's side.

With tears still rolling, Mr. Crenshaw allowed a hint of a smile to touch his lips. "Now that is what I call a strike. Good job, Maggie," Mr. Crenshaw squeezed her shoulder.

"Do you think he'll die?" Maggie asked.

Mr. Crenshaw paused before he answered. "From your bowling pin? No, Maggie. He might feel like he is dying, and he is as good as dead, but not from your mighty swing. He will stand trial, he will be found guilty, and he will hang. Best of all, I will be there to watch."

Thomas Gatlin moaned.

Maggie looked up at Mr. Crenshaw. He looked so forlorn. "Mr. Crenshaw? Are you going to be okay?"

"Ah, Maggie. You are truly a precious jewel as well as a fresh breath of air." He sighed, "In time, Maggie. In time, I'll be fine." Thomas Gatlin made a clumsy move for the shotgun.

It was Mr. Crenshaw's turn to laugh. "Go ahead, Thomas. It's a double barrel, and you've already fired twice which means it is empty. My gun is not, and I would take great pleasure in proving it to you."

CHAPTER 16

Orphanage or Workhouse?

"Mr. Crenshaw," Maggie said in an urgent tone. "Cecil and Elbert weren't in the basement where I thought they would be. Neither were Jed and Jess."

"Jed and Jess?" Mr. Crenshaw asked with a confused frown.

"I made them a promise," Maggie spread her hands wide to explain. "That's why I couldn't tell you before now."

"Promises are important to keep," he assured her.

"I've been hearing that a lot lately," Maggie sighed. She would never underestimate a promise again. "I think Mr. Gatlin knows where we can find the boys."

As Thomas Gatlin lay on the floor, Mr. Crenshaw stood over him and studied his bloody face. "Is that right, Thomas? Do you know where they are?"

Maggie watched the spark ignite in Mr. Gatlin's eyes. Now he had bargaining power. He wiped his bloody hand across his shirt and pulled himself into a sitting position. "You bet I know where they are, and if you don't agree to take me to the bank, I'll let them die right where they were left."

"What if I shoot you?" Mr. Crenshaw aimed his .38 Special.

Mr. Gatlin laughed. "Think, Arnold. What have I got to lose? If I go to trial I am already a dead man, and there is no way under heaven I'll spend another night in that mental ward at Larned. You wouldn't believe the endless screaming or the way a patient is treated there. No, you have more to lose than I do. If you want those horrible boys, and if you want me out of your life, we'll make a trip to the bank."

"Really?" Mr. Crenshaw frowned. "Maggie, forgive me, but will you just turn your back for a moment? This thing I am going to do is not a very Godly action." Mr. Crenshaw waited for Maggie to turn away.

"Now, then, Thomas, I didn't say I was going to kill you. I'm thinking about just shooting you in the leg. I'm thinking if that doesn't make you talk, then I'll shoot you in the other leg," Mr. Crenshaw spoke in a convincing tone.

Mr. Gatlin studied him. "You don't have the guts."

Maggie couldn't believe what she was hearing. She jumped and swirled around when the gun went off.

Mr. Thomas Gatlin clutched his leg as he rolled himself into a tight ball. He spewed words Maggie was ashamed to hear.

"Thomas, you are right," Mr. Crenshaw said firmly. "A few days ago I wouldn't have had the guts, but you killed my wife. You made her do awful things, and then you shot her. You tried to kill Maggie, not once but twice, and I have no idea what you've done with the boys."

Sweat was pouring through Mr. Gatlin's fingers. "So you would kill me and go to prison?"

"After what you did to Louise and Maggie, do you really think any jury would send me to prison? Thomas Gatlin, you disgust me. When you calm down, you'll see that I didn't shoot you. I shot into the air to scare you. I don't know what you felt, but it sure wasn't a bullet in your leg."

Maggie breathed a sigh of relief. She hadn't wanted to think that Mr. Crenshaw would do such a thing—even to that evil Mr. Thomas Gatlin.

Thomas Gatlin's eyes narrowed like the slits of a rattler's eyes. The air was thick with hatred.

Mr. Crenshaw aimed again. "Do you want me to shoot this time for real?"

"Don't shoot!" Mr. Gatlin spat. "Those brats are in the basement."

Maggie thought about being down there earlier. An eerie feeling swept over her as she swallowed dryly, "I was down in the basement, and no one was there."

Suddenly they all heard someone step onto the front porch.

Mr. Gatlin sneered triumphantly. "Come on in, Stub!"

Her eyes as wide as saucers, Maggie looked at Mr. Crenshaw. It couldn't be Stub, could it? Hadn't he run out of the mansion like a wild man? Surely he wouldn't have come back. Maggie watched as Mr. Crenshaw swung his pistol to cover the doorway.

Thomas Gatlin took the opportunity to lunge toward Maggie and pull her to the floor with him. "Put the gun down here on the floor, Arnold, or I'll break her little neck."

Slowly Mr. Crenshaw laid his gun down.

"Now kick it over to me." Thomas Gatlin growled as he struggled to stand while holding Maggie in his grasp. The hardwood floor where Gatlin had fallen earlier was splattered with gold coins just like the coin she had found earlier in the basement and had stashed in her pocket. Maggie gasped. So it did have something to do with Thomas Gatlin!

The door in the foyer swung wide. Stub Huggins stumbled into the house with his hands held high. Behind him, Maggie's daddy pushed Stub with the barrel of his gun.

Thomas Gatlin had his back to the foyer and didn't see that Maggie's daddy had come in behind Stub. "Come get the girl, Huggins. She must have nine lives. Take her to the basement, and this time make sure she's dead," Thomas Gatlin ordered.

Gatlin shoved Maggie at Stub, but Stub had spotted the gold. "My money!" Stub hungrily scooped up the coins and scrambled to collect more.

Not taking his eyes off Mr. Crenshaw, Gatlin yelled, "It isn't your money, Huggins! It's mine! Now take care of the girl!"

Stub continued to scrounge for coins like a chicken in search of grubs.

Sam grabbed Stub by the collar and tossed him across the room where he bounced against the wall and dropped to the floor. Then Sam dove on Thomas Gatlin, rolled him over, and slammed his face with his fist as Maggie scrambled out of the way. Sam was still pounding Gatlin when Sue, Opal, Ruby, and Martin flooded into the room.

Sue ran to Sam and pulled him away from Thomas Gatlin. "Stop it, Sam. You'll kill him."

Thomas Gatlin lay sprawled limply on the floor. Maggie didn't know if he were dead or alive. She grabbed Sue's hand and pointed to Mrs. Crenshaw's body.

Sue gasped. "Martin, take Opal and Ruby into the other room and keep them there."

With the commotion, no one heard the noise from the porch, but all were relieved when they saw Sheriff Ary, followed by Mrs. Valina, enter the mansion. Mrs. Valina grabbed the sides of her face with her hands. "I declare! What's happened here?"

Sheriff Ary was silent a moment before he took charge. "Martin, Valina can stay with the girls while you pull Sam's wagon up to the porch. It looks like we'll be needing it." Sheriff Ary walked over to Thomas Gatlin and stared at him. "I guess you're still alive." He then turned to Sam, "Have you arrested him yet?"

Sam rubbed his bloody fist, "I was getting to it."

Sheriff Ary raised his eyebrows. "So I see. I hope you don't ever have to arrest me."

Sam's lips twitched into a slight grin. "I don't reckon you will ever mess with my family."

The sheriff rubbed his chin. "Can't say as I blame you, but in this job, Sam, you have got to have control." Sam nodded his head. Sheriff Ary glanced about the room. "Let's move into the parlor, so everybody can sit down while I take some statements."

"First, we have to find the boys. He knows where they are, but he won't tell." Maggie pointed to the battered face of Thomas Gatlin.

Sheriff Ary stood over Thomas Gatlin. "Where are they?" the sheriff demanded.

Thomas Gatlin glared. "I want my money! Give me my money, and I'll tell you where the boys are."

"What money?" the sheriff asked.

Maggie stepped forward. "I think it's money like this." She pulled the gold coin from her pocket. "I found it under the steps in the basement near an old rusty box. When Mr. Gatlin fell on the floor, it looked like a bunch of the coins fell out of his pocket, but Stub has them all now."

"Stub?" the sheriff's eyes travelled to Huggins.

"Them is my coins. I dug 'em up, and they be mine! Gatlin took 'em and hid 'em!" Stub hissed.

Gatlin clenched his teeth. "It was my map. I found it in my granddad's papers when I was looking for that stupid will. That means the money is mine."

"Thomas, why would your granddad bury money?" asked Sheriff Ary.

"He didn't trust banks, that's why." Thomas sneered.

Sheriff Ary laughed. "Thomas, your granddad owned the bank. Or maybe that's why he didn't trust banks?"

As the laughter settled, Sheriff Ary rubbed his chin with a glint in his eye. "So, Stub, did you happen to dig them coins up from behind the Daniels' barn one dark night?"

Stub growled. "It ain't nobody's business where I dug them from!"

"I'll take that as a 'yes'," Sheriff Ary chuckled. "And that must be why Thomas wanted Sue's pasture for a hundred bucks." The sheriff held up a coin and studied it. "Why, one of these coins alone is probably worth at least a hundred! Sue, that makes you a wealthier woman than anyone thought."

Maggie's eyes sparkled. "Wait until Opal finds out there really was a treasure!"

"Now, Stub, where are the boys?" Sheriff Ary called over his shoulder.

Thomas sneered. "He doesn't know."

Stub spat a stream of tobacco juice past Thomas Gatlin's head. "He wouldn't tell me, and he had my money and my

scattergun. Now things are different. If someone will give me a knife and let me alone with this animal, I'll get it from him."

Sheriff Ary shrugged. "It's up to you, Thomas."

"You can't do that! It's not legal!"

"Neither is killing people," Mr. Crenshaw answered. "Sheriff, I'll be glad to get the knife."

Mr. Thomas Gatlin saw the hardened faces glaring at him, and fear stabbed his heart. "They're in the walk-in cooler down in the basement."

"The cooler?" Maggie gasped. "That will kill Jess. I think he has dust pneumonia!"

Mr. Crenshaw and Maggie ran to the landing, flipped on the gas lights, and flung the door open that led to the basement. Maggie scampered down first, but Mr. Crenshaw beat her to the cooler.

"OH! NO! There's a padlock on the door!" He yanked at it a few times. "Somebody get me a key!" Mr. Crenshaw yelled.

Maggie didn't have one, but she remembered the miner's pick that Stub Huggins had launched into the darkness when he fled up the basement stairs. With the light streaming in through the open door to the hallway, she was able to find it quickly. She dragged it across the floor to Mr. Crenshaw.

"Stand back, Maggie." He sliced the pick down on the lock and split it apart. Then he clasped the handle and pulled the door open. Four shivering boys stumbled out of the dark, damp, thick-walled cooler.

Through chattering teeth, Jed was the first to speak. "I knew you'd come, Maggie. Cecil said you would, too. We kept telling Jess and Elbert you'd be here."

"And you brought help," Elbert was hugging Mr. Crenshaw. Maggie kicked at the floor with the toe of her shoe. "I'm sorry I broke my promise, Jed. I finally had to tell Mr. Crenshaw. I needed help, and I just had to," Maggie begged. "Jed, Cecil, will you forgive me? Will you still trust me?"

"Trust you? Why, we just trusted you with our lives," Cecil spat on the basement floor. "I reckon your promise is as good as any guy's."

"I don't think you know what all Maggie went through to keep her promise to you," Mr. Crenshaw said. "She's a true friend. You have a lot to thank her for."

Maggie was concerned. "How is Jess?"

"Hey, you were right. The honey worked on his cough, and there was plenty of chicken broth in the pantry," Jed reported. "He was doin' pretty good until Gatlin locked us in there." He pointed to the cooler. Jed trembled as he turned to look nervously at Mr. Crenshaw. "He won't report us, will he, Maggie?"

"To whom?" Mr. Crenshaw asked.

Maggie answered. "They don't want to go to an orphanage or a workhouse."

"I see. Well, we'll talk about that later. Right now let's go upstairs."

Mrs. Valina had removed the dust sheets from the furniture in the parlor so everybody could sit down while they gave their statements to Sheriff Ary. The only place left to sit for Maggie and the boys was on the floor. Mr. Thomas Gatlin and Stub Huggins were handcuffed and sitting back to back on the rug in the center of the room. Martin had brought in extra chairs for himself and Mrs. Valina. Sheriff Ary stood in the entryway between the parlor and the dining room where Mrs.

Crenshaw's body lay. The sheriff wanted to keep all the kids from wandering in and seeing her. Sam sat on the edge of his seat ready for anything that might happen.

"Arnold and Maggie, I need your statements so we can wrap things up here," said Sheriff Ary.

Maggie poured out her story. The events of the evening seemed a lifetime long. Opal and Ruby squeezed close to Maggie. Sue wrapped her arms tightly about herself as a grim line formed on her lips. Sam's knuckles were white. Martin glared at the two handcuffed men.

Mrs. Valina shook her head in disbelief, all the while praying for God's favor as Mr. Crenshaw confirmed everything Maggie said.

The room became still as Maggie spoke almost in a whisper about how Mrs. Crenshaw had jumped in front of the shotgun to save Mr. Crenshaw. Tears streamed down the faces of everyone except Mr. Thomas Gatlin and Stub Huggins.

Mr. Crenshaw's voice broke, "When I was holding Louise in my arms, she told me she did that because of Maggie's mustard seed."

"Mustard seed?" asked Sheriff Ary.

Maggie blinked. "My mama, Sue, told me that asking the God up in heaven to live in your heart was like planting a mustard seed. A tiny mustard seed will grow into the biggest and strongest of all the trees. It will even offer shelter to others. When the God up in heaven lives in your heart, He grows there and helps you to be strong so you can help others. A lot of people keep the mustard seed in their hands and never plant it in their hearts."

Sue squeezed Maggie's hand and smiled.

After the Dust Settles

Piercing the broken hearts of the group gathered in the parlor, a low eerie moan floated from somewhere nearby. Stub Huggins's eyes nearly popped out of his head. "Get me out of this haunted place!" he yelled. Stub scrambled to his knees and struggled to crawl with handcuffed hands to the door. Sam quickly jumped up and grabbed him, dragging him back to the center of the parlor floor. The eerie moan filtered through the air once again, only this time it was louder, and there was no doubt it came from the dining room.

A startled Sheriff Ary swiftly turned to look behind him. It wasn't just Stub Huggins who was breaking out in a cold sweat. The whole group sat with wide eyes. Ruby broke the stunned silence as she pointed toward the dining room. "Who's in there?"

Opal looked to the door. "I ain't going to go look. You can if you want to, Ruby, but you'll go alone."

Slowly, Mr. Crenshaw turned to the door. The heartbreak he had felt since the shooting suddenly changed as his mouth dropped open. "Louise? It can't be!" He took long running strides into the dining room and knelt beside his wife. Gently he picked her up and cradled her in his arms. "You're not dead!" He turned to the group. "She's not dead! There's a lot of blood, but it looks like the bullet just creased her shoulder," he cried.

Louise moaned again and fluttered her eyes open. "Arnold Jack, you've ruined your clothes. Why, you have gotten blood all over them."

Mr. Crenshaw laughed. "I know, Louise. It will have to come out of my wages, but first we need to get you to the doctor."

"Dr. Nelson will charge extra for waking him in the night," Louise warned as she sank heavily in her husband's arms.

"Louise, I thought you were dead!" cried Mr. Crenshaw.

143

Louise smiled. "I think I must have fainted dead away. There seems to be a lot of blood, but I'm really not hurt that badly."

Maggie marveled at the love Mr. Crenshaw still held for Mrs. Crenshaw. She guessed it must have come from the God up in heaven.

Sheriff Ary pulled out his pocket watch and flipped the lid open. "Three o'clock in the morning. Louise needs a doctor. I guess we had better wind this up."

Maggie turned around just in time to see Jed nudge Jess and motion toward the door. Maggie guessed what they were planning, and she had to stop them. She didn't even want to think about them living in that old dugout. "Sheriff, what about Jed and Jess? What is going to happen to them?"

Jed stared at Maggie. He couldn't believe she was betraying them as they tried to sneak out the door.

Sheriff Ary pursed his lips together. "I don't rightly know. I'll have to contact the state, but rest assured somebody will take good care of them."

Jed stood and pulled Jess to his feet. "We ain't goin' to no orphanage, and we ain't goin' to no workhouse. Come on, Jess, let's hightail it out of here." Jess started coughing.

Sue stood, crossed to the boys, and put her arm around Jess's shoulders. "Jed, your brother needs some care. How about if the two of you come home with us?"

Jed squinted at Sue. "You ain't got no room in that boxcar. Besides, you'd just be keepin' us until the state got their paws on us."

"No, Jed," she shot a glance at Sam. "It wouldn't be just until the state comes to take you away. It would be for as long as you want to stay. It would be forever."

"Sue?" Sam looked at her.

"Where? Where would you put us?" Jed asked.

Sue smiled, "I was thinking of moving. I was actually thinking of moving right here into the Gatlin mansion. After all, I am part owner, and Thomas isn't going to be around to object."

Mr. Thomas Gatlin protested, "It will be a cold day … "

"Watch the language. There are ladies present," Sheriff Ary nudged him with Stub Huggins's shotgun.

Thomas Gatlin didn't stop talking, but he did clean up his language. "I will sign this place over to the state before I let you have it," he threatened.

Mr. Crenshaw smiled. "You can't. Your father's will states that if anything happens to you, everything goes to Sue's husband, and since she is his heir, it goes to her."

"I'll fight it in court!" Gatlin yelled.

"From prison?" Mr. Crenshaw asked. "From the gallows?"

Mr. Thomas Gatlin's face turned red with rage. "Louise, tell them … "

"No, Thomas." Louise struggled to speak. "I'll not cover for you ever again."

"You … you … " Thomas didn't finish.

Sheriff Ary held his gun over Gatlin. "Remember the ladies, Thomas."

"That's the Louise I married," Mr. Crenshaw smiled.

Sue turned to Sam, "I would like to turn this place into a boys' home. We could take in Jed and Jess, and if Mr. Crenshaw needs us to help out while Louise recovers, we'll take Cecil and Elbert, too. Is that okay, Sam?"

Sam shrugged. "I always did want a son or two or three or four, so I guess it would be fine."

"Martin and I can help," Mrs. Valina beamed. "We love children."

Sheriff Ary chuckled, "Now Mrs. Valina, you help these folks. However, Sam, Sue, don't ever let her drive. Whoever put Mrs. Valina in that auto didn't tell her how to stop the thing. She smashed it into my office wall. Now I need a new wall, and Arnold needs a new Model T!"

"Sheriff, you know that was an accident." Mrs. Valina propped her hands firmly on her hips. Sheriff Ary laughed.

Daddy and Sue turned again to Jed and Jess. "Would you two come and live with us?"

Jess nodded, but Jed walked over to his father who was still sitting in the middle of the floor. "Pa?"

Stub dropped his head and looked at his cuffed hands. "I wish you'd do it, Jed. I done made some bad promises to the wrong person. By the time I see the light of day, you'll be done grown." Jed nodded.

"We'll take good care of them, Stub," Sam said.

"And that's a promise," Sue added.

Mrs. Valina's wide smile spread to everyone in the room. "When this family makes a promise, you can take it to heaven with you and cash it in."

"Well, now that everything is settled, let's get these prisoners to jail, and I guess we'll have to wake up Dr. Nelson to see to our wounded. I doubt Thomas will bleed to death from the wounds on that face of his, so we'll ask Dr. Nelson to fix up Mrs. Crenshaw first."

Sheriff Ary paused, "At least Mrs. Valina left my prison bars still standing. You know, I may have to arrest her for destroying public property."

"Now, Sheriff, I done told you it was an accident, and you know it!" Mrs. Valina shook her finger and scolded him.

The Gatlin mansion filled with more laughter than it had seen since the peanut butter and honey sandwich party.

"Boys?" Sue asked. "Do we have a deal?" Jed was the first to stretch out his hand. Jess followed, with Cecil and Elbert right behind.

"Does this mean they are our brothers?" Opal asked with a hint of disgust.

All four boys surrounded her. "Yep," they said in chorus. Maggie noticed Opal was blushing. Maybe she did like Cecil just a bit.

Opal asked another question, "And are we all going to be living right here in the Gatlin mansion?"

Sue nodded.

Maggie wrapped her arms around herself. This mansion was going to be her home. She let her eyes travel about the people the God up in heaven had given her. She had come to Dodge City, Kansas, with just her daddy. Now she had a mama, sisters, brothers, and a whole slew of friends. Wow! The God in her heart was good.

Ruby gasped, "Does that mean I get the yellow room?"

"Not if I get there first," Opal laughed. All three sisters ran for the stairs.

A sense of warmth surged through Maggie. She didn't really want the yellow room, but as she ran up the steps, Maggie knew she had already told Ruby she would share it with her. It wasn't a promise, and she was glad. Promises given too freely were sometimes hard to keep.

Opal was faster than the other girls. Maggie giggled when Opal opened the wrong door to the room she had claimed.

Ruby shot past her to the yellow room. "The yellow room is mine! Mine and Maggie's!" Ruby called.

"Aw, bugs!" Opal groaned. "Two against one ain't fair, and I am the oldest!"

"But Maggie's older than you!" Ruby planted herself just inside the yellow room.

Maggie left them to the argument she knew they would have. She flew up the stairs to her favorite place in the whole mansion, the ballroom. She wanted to see how the colors from the stained glass windows lit the glassy floor in the moonlight. The beautiful colors were soft and dreamy. Maggie danced to the center of the pastel patch, swinging gracefully, and sank to the floor. She closed her eyes to dream of the Christmas plaid dress. She had desired it before she had ever been in this wonderful mansion, but now the desire of her heart was within reach of her finger tips. Excitement tingled through her body like fireworks. She was here, just where the God up in heaven had placed her. She would wrap her arms about the Gatlin porch pillars and climb over the porch railing just as she had dreamed. Even better, she would wear that Christmas plaid dress and dance in this same beautiful ballroom spotlighted by the moon. She loved this place she would call home. Maggie raised her head and thanked the God up in heaven.

Settlers fear the Shawnee Indians at Chillicothe.
Joshua is about to learn why.

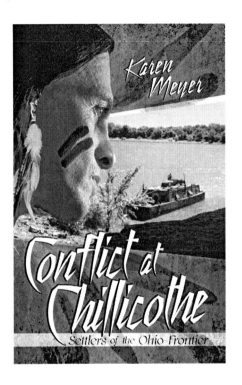

Karen Meyer

Conflict at Chillicothe

Settlers of the Ohio Frontier

For Joshua Stewart and his family, the
Kentucky frontier is their promised land.
It's a fresh start away from the difficulties
of Virginia. It's an opportunity to own as
much land as they care to claim. It's a
chance of a lifetime, a dream come true.

The only problem is getting there.

Experience the **Miracle** of a **Life** Completely Surrendered to the **Lord**

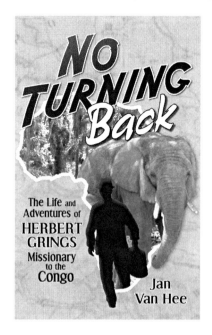

Herbert Grings was an ordinary man, but he accomplished extraordinary things. Read the compelling, true drama of a man who dedicated his life to spreading God's Word throughout the Belgian Congo of Africa. Whether you are struggling with your faith, have fully dedicated yourself to the Lord or are somewhere in between, the story of Herbert Grings is one that you must read!

LaVergne, TN USA
03 September 2010
195837LV00001B/4/P